# DANIEL MIGNAULT & JACKSON

— AS SEEN IN BUZZFEED AND THE HUFFINGTON POST —

Praise for *TITAN: The Gods War, Book I:*

"[Co-authors Daniel Mignault & Jackson Dean Chase have] stepped up to the plate with gusto...[a] diligently crafted debut novel..."
— The Huffington Post

"[*Titan*] succeeds in taking fiction to a whole new level."
— TheBaynet.com

"Irresistible... a heart-pounding story full of suspense, romance, and action!" — Buzzfeed

"Excellent... *Titan* is a beautifully crafted story that braves all odds."
— Medium.com

"...[loaded with] suspense, romance, and action thrills."
— The Odyssey Online

"A delectably great experience... [gives urban fantasy] a new twist."
—ThriveGlobal.com

"...will keep readers guessing until the very end."
— WN.com

First Printing, July 2018

ISBN-13: 978-1723315435 / ISBN-10: 1723315435

Published by Jackson Dean Chase, Inc.

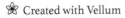 Created with Vellum

# KINGDOM OF THE DEAD

THE GODS WAR — BOOK II

## DANIEL MIGNAULT
## JACKSON DEAN CHASE

WWW.JACKSONDEANCHASE.COM

*For the man who released the Kraken,*
*RAY HARRYHAUSEN (1920-2013)*

*The magic remains... the monsters too.*

# A NOTE FROM THE AUTHORS

## IF YOU HAVE NOT READ BOOK 1 IN THIS SERIES

Welcome, citizen! This is Book 2 in our epic urban fantasy series, *The Gods War*. It assumes you have read and are familiar with the characters, events, and world described in Book 1: *Titan*. If you have not read the first book, we strongly recommend you STOP NOW, go back, and read *Titan* before reading this one. Not only will it give you a better understanding of this book, it will substantially increase your enjoyment of it, as well as prevent you from stumbling across MAJOR SPOILERS for the first book.

But if you want to read the series out of order, or if it's been a while since you read *Titan*, we've included a glossary in the back (be aware it contains SPOILERS for Book 1).

With that out of the way, let us tell you a story: the story of a cruel and magical future, a world ruled by monsters of Greek Myth. It is a dystopian world, a near-future nightmare that is part ancient Greece, part modern day America. And it is the world our heroes want to save. Come then, if you dare! Come and face the darkness within us, and within you...

— DANIEL MIGNAULT & JACKSON DEAN CHASE

# KINGDOM OF THE DEAD

Only the dead have seen the end of war.

— George Santayana

# A HISTORY OF GODS AND TITANS

AS TAUGHT BY THE PRIESTS OF THE NEW GREEK THEOCRACY

IN THE BEGINNING, all was Chaos. From that primal Chaos sprang Gaia, the Earth Mother, and Ouranos, the Sky Father. From the holy union of Heaven and Earth came their children, the immortal Titans. But Ouranos grew jealous of his children and cast them into Tartarus, the vast and terrible underworld. There, the Titans languished until Cronus, the youngest and most daring of them, escaped. Cronus defeated Ouranos, and there was much rejoicing as the Titans were reunited with Gaia.

There was a Golden Age of peace under the rule of Cronus, King of the Titans, and his queen, Rhea. But when Rhea became pregnant, Cronus knew he could not let his spawn usurp him as he had usurped his own father.

Cronus devoured his children. One after the other: Hades, Hera, Hestia, Demeter, and Poseidon. But not Zeus. Rhea had had enough of her children being devoured when she became pregnant with Zeus, so she hid him away and substituted a rock disguised to look like a child in his place. Cronus ate the rock, and it joined the children in his stomach who were still alive, being digested for all eternity.

These children were a new race, a lesser race called Gods, but they could not die. So mighty Cronus swallowed them, not only to ensure they would never escape, but also to absorb their power and add it to his own...

Zeus decided to overthrow Cronus. Zeus was a cowardly, deceitful creature who lacked the power to challenge his father directly. He knew he could never do it alone, so he poisoned Cronus, which caused him to vomit up his imprisoned brothers and sisters.

The Gods then went to war against the Titans and after ten long years, managed to imprison them in Tartarus. And Zeus, the youngest of the Gods, became their ruler, much as Cronus had when he overthrew Ouranos...

But Zeus was a pretender! He and his fellow Gods thought they could rule better than the Titans, but they could not. Because they had been held so long in Cronus's stomach, all the Gods except Zeus needed the psychic power of others. So the Gods created mankind to worship them, and they made us in their own image, but they knew better than to make us immortal. They thought we would worship them forever, and for a time we did, in many countries under many names, but the Gods grew complacent and our faith waned.

That waning faith is what caused the locks imprisoning the Titans in Tartarus to weaken. And then the locks broke and the Titans were released, igniting the Gods War. A war the Gods could not win, and when they refused to surrender, they were responsible for why so much of our world was destroyed.

The Titans won, and rather than make the mistake of keeping the Gods in Cronus's stomach again, the Titans had them killed, all of them except Hades... The Titans kept the God of Death alive, but imprisoned in Tartarus, so we mortals could never die. That was the Titans' gift, the Titans' promise!

But life without purpose is life not worth living. So in their mercy, the Titans created the New Greece Theocracy from the ashes of the American west coast. And in our great country, our proud and undying NGT, they allowed mankind to serve their infinite glory forever.

*All hail the Titans! All hail the NGT!*

# PART I

TO FIGHT A TITAN

# 1

## INTO THE UNDERWORLD

THIS IS WHAT IT'S LIKE TO BE DEAD. It's funny, but it's true. I'm in the boat of Charon—just like a dead man, like a ghost, a ferried soul on its final journey. I hope this won't be mine. There are people I love, people I care for back on Earth. I can't let them down, just like I can't let my friends down: Mark Fentile and Hannah Stillwater. They're in the boat with me, my fellow fugitives from life, from death, from horror.

How we got here, to this place between worlds, is a long story. I go over it in my mind, searching for answers, searching for truth among the lies, the magic, the mystery. Maybe, if I can wrap my head around it, it will all make sense. Maybe I won't feel so lost or alone, though I don't know why.

I've always felt this way.

The River Styx flows, and we flow with it. Down, into the deep. Down, into the underworld, to Tartarus, the Kingdom of the Dead. But Tartarus is not just home to ghosts, it is home to monsters and to Hades, Greek God of Death. He has been imprisoned by Cronus, King of the Titans. Cronus the Immortal. Cronus the Cannibal, All-Devouring Father of the Gods: Zeus, Poseidon, and all the rest. Cronus, who is my father too.

My name is Andrus Eaves. I only discovered the truth of my birth yesterday... That I was born from a rock. The magic rock Cronus ate, tricked into thinking it was his son, Zeus. The rock that absorbed a fraction of my father's power. Power that flowed into me and *became me.*

In my former life, I was the adopted son of George and Carol Eaves. The Eaves are rich from oil—oil I found as a child in our backyard. That's another of my gifts, sensing the bounty of the earth. But my old life, my old esteemed position in society is gone. I wanted to join the Warrior caste and serve the New Greece Theocracy, the NGT that rules what's left of Earth. I wanted to put in my military service helping my fellow citizens before joining the family oil business. That's hard to do when you're on the run.

The NGT wants me dead.

That's because Cronus doesn't want any more children. *Especially me.* He likes to eat his spawn because, well, you know the story: Cronus worries they will grow up to challenge him. And he's right—I know I will. And I know Zeus did, and won, for a time. Only Zeus is dead. The Gods are dead: dead or fled, fled and gone. Only Hades remains, imprisoned in the depths of Tartarus. That's where Hannah, Mark, and I are going. To free her father.

*To free Hades.*

I look to Charon, the robed and hooded figure in black who guides our boat down the Styx. He's a living mummy, with parchment-thin flesh stretched tight over ancient bones. But he's not without a sense of style: his pointed beard is groomed into shape with cobwebs. And Charon's boat is just as ghoulish: long and narrow, like a gondola, decorated with the bones and skulls of the dead. Not exactly cheery, but at least it's consistent and exactly what you'd expect from the Ferryman of Souls.

I look to my friend, Mark Fentile, former priest-in-training. Mark, one step up from slavery, so poor he had to live in Loserville. Poor Mark! All he ever wanted was to serve the Titans and the Theocracy. That was before he realized how evil they are.

Mark has lost everything: his alcoholic mother, hung by the neck in their Loserville shack. Lucy, his beautiful blonde sister—*the girl who dared to love me*—lost to the clutches of our enemy, Inquisitor Anton.

Mark's mother is a zombie now, and Lucy, we don't know what happened to her. We only know she sacrificed herself wounding Anton, to buy Mark and I time to get to Hannah, and to buy herself revenge on Anton for raping her. I hope Lucy is OK, because if she isn't, she might be a zombie now too.

That's because the dead don't die. Not as long as Hades is imprisoned. Once King of Tartarus, now he is its prisoner, and a prisoner cannot force the dead to die. So the dead live on, in mindless agony, as zombies.

Immortality is the Titans' "gift" to humanity, the gift the Gods never gave, and now we know the reason why. It's a curse. You grow up, aging normally, then when you hit adulthood, you don't stop, but slow down—so slow, each year is like a decade, and that's great until you get too old to function. Then you slowly wither, yet horribly go on. That's because unlike the Gods or Titans, the human body isn't meant to live forever. But the bodies of immortals? Bodies like mine? We go on. We must go on until we are destroyed or destroy ourselves.

Like I intend to destroy Cronus—with Hades' help, and the help of my friends. Once Hades is free from his prison, then even Gods and Titans can die...

I look to Hannah Stillwater, the beautiful witch, the Demigoddess. She's thin, black-haired, and pale, wearing a purple cloak and toga. Almost eighteen, like Mark and me. Her dark eyes are tombstone gray and sharp with intelligence. Her raven familiar, Shadow, sits perched on her shoulder.

I look behind us, to the shores of the secret cave below Bronson Canyon. In the past, before the Gods War, the canyon was a place of magic and monsters. Hollywood filmed everything from *Batman* to *It Conquered the World* there. Under the NGT, it's a place of magic and monsters again, only this time, it's all real and nowhere is safe.

Moments ago, we barely got away from Captain Nessus and his

Night Patrol: centaurs and harpies. We'd still be fighting them if I hadn't used my magic to collapse the tunnel behind us.

So that's where my life's at. It's easy to look back, to other people, other places. It's not so easy to look to yourself, to gaze deep inside, but that's what I do now, and it all comes down to this:

*I am Andrus Eaves.*

*I am a Titan, and I am Earth's last hope.*

# 2

---

THE PLAN

OUR BOAT GLIDES ON, through the murky darkness, through black, sluggish water. All around us is rock. Rock walls, rock ceiling. The Underworld. The Afterworld. Silent and eternal.

Tartarus is where your spirit goes when you die. It's not a place of punishment, it's just where the dead live. But just because you're dead doesn't mean you stop living—the flesh fails, but the spirit goes on. You're still you, only a ghost, and you go on doing the things you did in life. Sometimes good, sometimes bad. The difference is your mistakes can't kill you. You have eternity to learn and grow, to know joy or to suffer...

Hades ruled Tartarus once, and despite the Theocracy's propaganda, Hannah says he did a pretty good job. Now the Titans rule in his place. I'm not sure how things have changed, except there are probably more monsters. Monsters like harpies and centaurs need magic to breed, and there isn't enough of it on Earth. Oh, there's enough for short-term spells and the like, but long-term, sustained magic is hard unless you're a God or Titan. That's why monsters died out in the past. They're sterile on Earth.

Tartarus on the other hand, well, this place is pretty much *all magic*. It's below the Earth, but not really part of it: another dimension. You can only get in through gates, like the one we passed through back in Bronson Canyon.

The air down here isn't air at all. It's a deadly combination of sulphur, brimstone, methane, and other toxic things. As immortals, Hannah and I are immune. To me, the air has a strange, smokey flavor, but nothing too bad. But Mark is mortal, and shouldn't be able to breathe. He should be choking right now, strangling, becoming a zombie.

Only he isn't. He's wearing the ghost-mask Hannah gave him, a mask that makes Mark look like one of the dead, and allows him to breathe the gruesome gasses that fill Tartarus. "I can't believe it," Mark says. "We're really here, in the Underworld!"

Hannah shrugs. "It's not that special, priest. I grew up here. Personally, I couldn't wait to get out, but I guess every one feels the same about their home town. What about you, Rock Boy? You excited to be here?"

I bristle at the nickname. "I'm excited we're all in one piece. As for being here, well, it's better than being back there. I hope Ares is all right. Last I saw, Captain Nessus had his magic sword."

"Correction," Hannah says, "Nessus had *one* of his swords. You can bet Ares still has the other."

We'd left the God of War behind. Ares had bought us time to get inside the cave. I still can't get over the fact he was Mr. Cross, my gym teacher in disguise. No wonder he'd been so hard on me. He was secretly training me for this...

"You think we'll see him again?" I ask.

Hannah flashes a grim smile. "We're going to war, aren't we? War is kind of his thing. You can bet Ares will turn up sooner or later, don't worry."

I flash her a smile of my own. "Who's worried?"

"Don't try to play it off. You're worried as hell. We all are... Well, except this guy." She jerks her thumb back at the living mummy piloting the boat. "Charon's pretty chill, aren't ya?"

Charon bows his bony neck in a grisly nod. We sail on. Into the night. Into endless darkness.

I let the silence sink in, let it wash over me like waves. I reach out to the rocks we pass, taking comfort in them. Hannah's not wrong: *I am worried.* We're in danger: incredible, impossible danger! But we're also taking action. We're doing what's right. Right for us, and right for the world. Alone, none of us could, but together? We might have a shot.

"So what's the plan?" I ask Hannah. "You recruited us, remember?"

"Actually, I recruited *you*. I warned against involving Mark."

"I was already involved." Mark doesn't sound bitter, though he has every right to be. What he does sound is determined. "We're all in this together. I may be human, but I have something neither of you has."

"What's that?" Hannah asks.

"Brains."

She laughs. "Well, you're not stupid. I'll give you that."

"And you're brave," I tell him.

Mark shrugs. "I guess, but I'm not brave because I want to be. I'm brave because I have to."

"Not much difference in the end," Hannah muses. "We're all coming out of this heroes."

"Heroes or traitors," I remind her, "the biggest the world has ever seen."

She raises an eyebrow. "Oh, so you're bigger than Zeus now?"

"If we win, I am. If we win, Cronus is dead, the Titans are dead, and... well, I'm not sure what happens after that, but I'm sure it will be impressive. And we'll all be bigger than Zeus, not just me." I add that last part because it sounds crazy to put all this on me. Yet part of me, the newly awakened Titan part says, *Yes, I can defeat Cronus. Yes, I can save the world. I can rule in his place, because I should rule, only my rule will be just and strong and forever...*

Where is this coming from? I shake my head to clear it. I've had so many strange dreams, so many strange thoughts. It's my connection to Cronus. Through the accident of my birth, I absorbed part of his power, but what if I absorbed part of who he is as well? What if I'm no better than him and I just don't know it yet?

"The plan," I say, "what is it?"

Hannah shrugs. "To free my father."

"Yeah, you told us that, but how exactly? You do know where Hades is, don't you?"

Hannah chews her lower lip. "It's complicated; the location is cloaked by magic. Magic no immortal can see through except Cronus, since it's his spell."

"And me?" I ask. "You think I can because of my connection to him?"

She nods. "That's what Ares and I are hoping."

"OK, so how do I do it?"

"Um... you just close your eyes, reach out, and look for him."

"I look for him with my eyes shut?"

"Yes, genius! Look with your *mind's eye*. The magic of Tartarus will enhance whatever natural ability you have... if you have any."

"You can do it," Mark says. "Have faith!"

"Spoken like a true priest," Hannah jokes.

He looks away. "Well, I don't know about that. I'm kind of between deities right now."

I apologize. "Sorry, man. I didn't mean it like that. I mean, I appreciate your confidence in me. Both of you."

"Charon too," Hannah adds. "He may not look it, but he's cheering you on."

I look at the grim, skull-faced ferryman. He looks back, with empty, unknowable eyes. "Thanks," I tell him.

Charon gives me a stiff, creaking nod, then returns to staring straight ahead. I watch his pole go in the river, propelling our boat forward. Pole in, pole out.

I try to time my breath with the pole. Breathe in, breathe out. *Slowly.* I close my eyes. Relaxing, going inside myself. I listen to the sound of the boat, the river, the rustle of Charon's robe.

I reach out, sensing water, sensing rock: *the river, the tunnel.*

Forward motion: *slow, rhythmic.* Across the Styx, the River of Hate and Promises, and beyond... deep, into haunted Tartarus...

I sense the whispering presence of ghosts, but feel the physicality of monsters. Breath hot, muscles strong. Wild, animal, unnatural. *Magic.*

I feel other things too... brothers, sisters. *Titans.* Some monstrous, some fair, but all to be avoided. Unless... some of them want to rebel against Cronus? But no, as helpful as that would be, we can't risk it. Why should they follow me? I'm no one, nobody.

I pull away from them and keep searching, but it's no use. I don't know what to look for. I come back into myself, feeling drained.

"Any luck?" Hannah asks.

"None. Everything radiates magic, and I'm too new at this to know what to look for."

"The first time's always hard. Don't worry, you'll get better at it." She says it with a smile, but I can tell Hannah's not happy.

"I've let you down. I'm sorry."

"No," she says. "Not yet, you haven't."

We drift downriver, the only sound the creak of Charon's bones, the *slosh* of the pole dipping into the water. Maybe I can try again...

All of a sudden, Mark says, "Hey, wait! I've got an idea."

"Yeah?" I say. "What is it?"

"Maybe we're going about this the wrong way."

"Wrong way how?" Hannah asks.

"What if the problem isn't just that Andrus doesn't know what to look for, or that the whole underworld is covered in magic? What if instead of looking for the spell hiding Hades' prison, we should be looking for an area that *doesn't* look like magic?"

"You know I'm a witch, right?" Hannah reminds him. "I already tried that. I tried everything! I really thought Andrus might be able to succeed where I failed."

"Maybe it's impossible," Mark says.

Hannah snorts. "Really? That's a good attitude!"

"No," Mark says, "I didn't mean it like that. What if it's impossible for you, or Andrus, or anyone else to find Hades?"

"All right, maybe... but I don't see how giving up helps."

I've known Mark long enough to understand his moods, and how his devious mind works. "Hear him out," I say. "Go on, Mark."

He nods. "OK, so assuming Cronus's spell cloaks Hades' prison from immortals, what about mortals?"

"You mean you?"

Mark shakes his head. "No, not me. I mean monsters."

Hannah and I stare at each other, then Mark. "Even if that's true," she says, "the monsters are all on Cronus's side. They'll never agree to help us."

"I'm not talking about *any* monster," Marks replies. "I'm talking about one in particular. The one closest to Hades. The one guaranteed to be on our side and to know what to look for."

Hannah's face lights up. She leans over and hugs Mark, kissing him on the cheek as the thin boy blinks in surprise. "I love this mortal!" Hannah says, all trace of her bad mood gone. "Didn't I tell you it was a great idea to bring him?"

I scratch my head. "Wait, I don't get it... What monster are we looking for?"

"Cerberus," Hannah says. "We're looking for Cerberus."

# 3

WORTH A SHOT

"WHAT'S THE DEAL with this guy?" I ask Hannah, indicating the living mummy behind us. "Charon doesn't talk?"

The undead ferryman moves his withered head in my direction. The jaw clacks open and shut, but no sound comes out, just a faint puff of dust.

"He's telepathic," Hannah explains, "but only the dead hear him."

I frown, worried this piece of news will mess up the plan I've been forming. "You're not dead, can you hear him?"

"I'm the daughter of Hades, so I have a natural affinity for ghosts and other... things. So to answer your question, yes, I can hear him. Why do you ask?"

"Because we need to know where Cerberus is. I figured Charon must know."

"He doesn't. Charon only knows what's on or adjacent to the river. He has a bond with the water and the shore."

"Well, damn! That sucks. No offense. I was really hoping he could help."

"He *is* helping," Hannah says. "He's giving us a ride, remember?"

"Yeah, I know. I'm sorry. Just where are we going then, anyway?"

Hannah shrugs. "Wherever we want, as long as the Styx will take us there. The default destination is Customs and Immigration."

"What?"

"When you die, your ghost needs to get processed and accounted for, and to make sure you aren't trying to smuggle anything into Tartarus you shouldn't."

"Like what?" Mark asks.

"Like the living," Hannah replies. "That's another reason to keep that mask on. Tartarus is only for ghosts and monsters, and immortals, like me and Andrus. If anyone found out you were alive, Mark, they'd try to kill you, or..."

"Or what?" Mark asks.

"Or possess you to hitch a ride back to Earth."

"Right. Why would they try to kill me though? Because I'm alive and they're not?"

"Some would, but there's also a reward for killing trespassers. That way, if they turn you into a ghost, you can't leave and the secrets of Tartarus stay hidden."

"Great."

Hannah shrugs. "That's the way my father set it up, and the Titans saw no reason to change it. Even if the ghosts didn't try to kill or possess you, they'd bug you with all kinds of questions about what the world is like now, if you know their loved ones and can send a message, or take revenge for them, all the usual annoying ghost stuff. They'd follow you around, pestering and pleading, and that means we'd be attracting all kinds of attention."

"Mask on," Mark says. "Got it." We sail downriver for a few more minutes, then Mark snaps his fingers. "Hey! I know you said Charon only knows about the Styx, but does he ferry monsters as well as ghosts?"

"He ferries anyone who can pay. I mean, as long as it fits in the boat. He doesn't discriminate."

"OK," Mark says, "so maybe he overheard some monsters talking about Cerberus? Something that might give us a clue?"

Charon turns to Hannah, and I suspect he's using telepathy. My guess is confirmed a minute later when Hannah mods, then says, "Sorry, guys. Charon hasn't heard anyone talking about Cerberus, and wherever the Titans are keeping him, it's nowhere near the riverbanks."

Mark's shoulders slump. "Too bad. Well, it was worth a shot."

"I could try summoning some ghosts," Hannah says. "One of them might know."

"Too risky," Mark says. "What if they rat us out to Cronus?"

"The ghosts I'd summon would be my friends, like Herophilos, the doctor who treated Mark. They'd never betray me. That would be like betraying my father."

"You mean your father who's in prison and unable to help them?"

Hannah scowls.

"Wait," I say. Everyone stares at me, even Charon, though of course he doesn't have eyes. Whatever he's got, I can *feel* him looking at me.

"What's up?" she asks.

"Maybe... maybe we're asking the wrong question."

Hannah's brow furrows. "Wrong how? We need to find Cerberus, so it makes sense to ask about him."

"Yeah, but what if... well, Cronus wants me dead, and he knows— or at least suspects—you and I are working together."

"Right."

"I get it," Mark interrupts.

She frowns at him. "Get what?"

"I was on the right track," he replies, "but Andrus is right. It was the wrong question because it was too easy. With you involved, Cronus would guess we were coming to Tartarus. He'd make sure no one talked."

"Operational security," I explain, grateful I paid attention that day in warrior training class. "So no one is likely to have said anything, especially in the presence of Charon here, who was such a close ally of your father. And frankly, if they had, I'd suspect it was a trap."

"So what's the right question?" Hannah asks.

"Have there been any unusual troop movements lately?" I ask Charon. "Have you ferried anyone important, and to where?"

The undead ferryman nods. Hannah's eyes glaze over, going deep into thought as the mummy beams his reply into her brain. When her eyes snap back into focus, she grins. "Charon says he's seen troops marching along the bank toward the Garden of Bone."

I don't like the sound of that. "Garden of what now?"

"I'll tell you about it later. The main thing is we have a direction to go now. Oh, and Charon also confirms that he ferried a Titan the other day to join them."

"A Titan?" I say. "Which one? Not Cronus?"

"No, not Cronus. Nobody you've ever heard of. One of the Lesser Titans, the giants."

"You mean like a cyclops?" Mark asks.

"Worse," Hannah replies. "Gyges."

"*Guy-GHEZ?*" I stumble over the pronunciation. "What's a Gyges? I must have slept through that class."

"Not what," Hannah says. "*Who.* Gyges is one of the hundred-handers, three brothers who guard the gates of Tartarus."

Now it clicks. "Aren't they the ones with fifty heads? The ones who can throw a hundred rocks all at once?"

"They sure are. That means your earth magic is going to come in handy, pardon the pun." Her raven cackles at the joke.

I start to laugh too, then frown. "What do you mean, my earth magic?"

"Well, you have an affinity with rocks, so you'll figure something out. You better, or we're dead meat. Pounded meat, like hamburger."

"But I barely understand my power! What makes you think I can defeat that thing?"

"Gyges didn't spend years in Cronus' stomach, absorbing his powers. *You did.* That's what makes me think you can beat him, or at least hold him off long enough for Mark and me to rescue Cerberus."

I don't have a reply, just a sinking feeling our quest might be over before it's begun. I barely notice when Mark asks how a giant could fit in Charon's boat without sinking it. Hannah mutters something about magic, how most things can shrink to fit inside the boat, then return to their original size after they exit. Which makes as much sense as anything in this crazy, upside-down world.

# 4

## THE PILLARS OF ASH

To get to the Garden of Bone, we take a detour through the Pillars of Ash. It's a large cavern, miles long, with walls formed from basalt: volcanic black stone. And it's quiet, dark and deep, lit only by the orange glow of cinders—cinders set deep in the ashen pillars that rise smoky gray from beneath timeless black water.

The pillars reach like burnt fingers, ghostly and grasping toward the rock ceiling but never quite reaching their goal. The air smells of smoke. Smoke and sadness, the sorrow of charred dreams.

Charon stops poling the boat to breathe them in, or whatever passes for breath in his skeletal body. I hear him huff, see his chest inflate under his thick black robe. He doesn't exhale, but slowly his chest sinks back in. Whatever he did, it seems to strengthen him.

As we drift between the Pillars of Ash, Hannah explains they're made of trapped souls—all those who refuse to move on, who never achieved their dreams in life. They never reach the cavern's ceiling like they never reached anything in life. So they stay here and rot.

"There's no room for them in Tartarus," Hannah says. "They wander, hopeless and alone, ghosts even to other ghosts, then their souls just burn out and blow away, binding to these pillars."

"Why?" Mark asks.

"Because even in death, like seeks like. These souls represent life's losers."

Mark grimaces at the word. As one of the poor, he'd been branded a Loser—with a capital "L"—and forced to live in Loserville, in the worst part of Othrys, the capital of the New Greece Theocracy.

Hannah notices Mark's reaction and quickly adds, "It's not about social caste or finances, of course. Their fate isn't based on what others branded them as in life, but on how they branded themselves in death."

"What do you mean?" Mark asks.

Hannah pauses, considering her answer, then says, "It's like if you die feeling worthless and unsatisfied, and don't believe you have a right to enjoy any kind of afterlife, then you end up here, in the Pillars of Ash. If you didn't, you'd just be clogging up the underworld and making everyone else's eternity miserable."

"So I'm not going to end up here?" Mark asks.

"Not unless you choose to."

"Good," Mark says. "There's no way I'd ever choose something like that."

Hannah shrugs. "You'd be surprised how many people do. I know it doesn't make sense, but that's just the way it is. You have to be your own savior; nobody can do it for you. Not Gods, not Titans. Only you. You decide where you go when you die, and what you get when you arrive."

I've been listening to the conversation, and now I have something to say, something I need to be clear on if we're going to free Hades and allow people to die again. "So let me see if I get this straight... You're telling me scumbag murderers like Anton get a free pass into Tartarus? I mean, if that's where they want to go?"

"No one gets in for free," Hannah says. "You have to pay Charon, but if a murderer was happy with his life or wanted to move on, he wouldn't be refused admission. If he was happy killing, he'd get assigned to Murder Town."

"Murder Town? That's great. Real cheery."

"It is, in a way. Murder Town is where all the killers and their victims go... if they're not ready to move on."

"Sounds horrible."

"It is, and it isn't. Remember, these souls *want* to be there, for whatever reason. And when they're ready to move on, they move on."

"To where? Prison?"

"If that's what they want. There are those who seek eternal torment and those who seek redemption. Hades gives the dead what they want, not necessarily what they *need*. If you ask for the wrong thing, well, that's what you get, and hopefully, you learn from it... It might take a hundred years, or a thousand, but most souls learn... eventually."

As we sail close to one of the smoky pillars, Charon reaches out a bony claw and scoops a fistful of ash from it. A few stray cinders fly away. The undead ferryman brings the ash to his mouth and eats it, staining his yellow teeth and leathery fingers soot-black.

I notice he doesn't eat the cinders; they break free and drift toward the ceiling as Hannah continues, "It's up to each soul, each ghost, to decide what's right for them. And it's not like they can't change their minds, so some choose to experience all kinds of things..."

I point up. "What about those cinders? The ones that just broke free?" I watch as they reach the volcanic ceiling, stick, then fade away.

Hannah cranes her neck to follow my finger. "Oh, those? They're souls who found hope and fanned it into a flame, ambition strong enough to break free and move on. When they reach the ceiling, they're sent to Tartarus for processing, just like any other newly arrived soul."

"So the Pillars aren't eternal punishment?" Mark asks.

"Nothing is, unless you want it to be." Her familiar caws and bobs its beak in agreement.

"And the souls Charon just ate?" I ask.

Hannah shrugs. "They were never going to break free. Charon simply ended their pain."

My jaw drops. "Seriously? By eating them?"

"By transferring their energy to something useful—*to him*. How else do you think a living mummy could get by? Especially one who poles a boat all day?"

"We all gotta eat," I agree, but it's more to be polite than anything. I flash Charon a smile—a smile that freezes on my face when I notice the soot marks on his teeth slowly absorb into him. His teeth are no longer yellow but gleaming white, the color of a carcass freshly picked clean.

"I'll be glad to get out of this place," Mark says.

"Yeah," I say. "Me too."

Hannah shakes her head. "Bit gloomy for you, huh? I thought you were a scholar, Mark? Don't you find all this interesting?"

"Oh, it's interesting," Mark says. "Maybe I'll feel more like studying it later. You know, when I'm dead."

"Plenty of time then," Hannah agrees. Unlike Mark and me, she isn't unsettled by this creepy stuff at all. And why should she be? She grew up here. Soul-eating mummies, hundred-handed giants, these are all normal to her, and maybe what's normal to us is weird to her.

And that makes me wonder... If I'd been raised here by Cronus, how different would I be? What makes a man a man, or a Titan a Titan? Is it nature or nurture? Or is it both? I don't have those answers, but I know I will by the time our quest is done. And that's what scares me. I've spent a lot of time lately wondering what I am, and now that I know, I wonder what kind of Titan I'll be...

I know there are good and bad examples, like Cronus, who would eat his own children, and Prometheus, who would help mankind by teaching them how to make fire. Not all the Titans sided with Cronus before, but those who defied him didn't end well. Zeus and the other Olympians seemed to have a short memory, and even shorter gratitude. Many of the Titans who sided with them had been betrayed. And yet here I am, a Titan, thinking of helping an Olympian... What other choice do I have?

I would never betray them, but after we succeed in defeating Cronus and the rest, what will stop Hades from betraying me? I look at Hannah and wonder. But it isn't Hannah or her father I have to worry about now. It's the menacing shape I see breaking the surface...

Before I can even get a warning out, the river monster raises its massive head, a head that looks like a melted crab crossed with a squid. A head attached to a long, eel-like body covered in spines and armor-like scales. It has dead black eyes on stalks, and four long whisker-like tentacles. They branch out from its upper lip, two to each side, each ending in a barbed stinger. The tentacles are translucent and gruesome green liquid pumps through the veins: poison to fuel the stingers. And the mouth... the mouth has teeth like daggers. It looks like a nightmare and sounds like a scream.

"Look out!" I cry as the monster rushes toward us. If it hits the boat, we'll be capsized, thrown into the inky water with it and no shore to swim to. But right before it hits us, the creature veers violently to the left and away. Our boat rocks a little in its wake, but that's it. I stare after the beast, wondering why it changed its mind, and if it will change it again and circle back.

"What the hell was that?" Mark demands. He's gone pale with fright and looks how I feel.

"Relax," Hannah says. "We're safe. It can't hurt us. Charon's boat is safe against attack from monsters or anything else. My dad laid the magic wards himself. Their protection is good for another thousand years, if not forever."

"You, uh, didn't mention there were river monsters," Mark says. "Is there anything else you haven't told us?"

Hannah smiles in reply. "If I'd stopped to warn you about everything we're going to meet, we'd still be back on the shore. You might not have even gotten in the boat."

"But we did," I say, "and I can see where the river monsters might have slipped your mind, seeing as how they can't hurt us."

"Exactly! As long as we stay in the boat, nothing can hurt us. Too bad we have to get out of it sometime."

"Yeah," I say. "Too bad." As we sail out of the cavern, I give a lingering look at the Pillars of Ash. There's no sign of the monster, and even the light of the cinders fades away.

*One monster down, a million more to go.*

# 5

WE'RE HEROES, RIGHT?

OUR BOAT'S BACK in the tunnels. Charon poles us along, faster now that he's fed. Above us, in the dark recesses of the ceiling, a curtain of cobwebs hangs down, sighing in the chill breeze like the tapestry to some forgotten dream.

I turn to watch the web after we pass, wondering.

Hannah raises an eyebrow. "Afraid of spiders?"

"Only giant ones."

She laughs. "Those are the ones to be afraid of."

"So, um... We won't have to pass through the gates of Tartarus to get to the Garden of Bone, will we? I don't want to deal with both of Gyges' brothers if we don't have to."

"We won't," Hannah says. "There's the front gate all the souls pass through—and most everyone else—and then there's the back gates only a few people know about. We're using one of those."

"How many secret gates are there?"

Hannah shoots me a look. "One, so far as you know."

"Who else knows about the gate? Does Cronus?"

"No, Andrus, Cronus doesn't know. He's not omniscient. He only knows what he sees for himself or what others tell him, as much as he'd like everyone to believe otherwise. That's not to say he isn't incredibly clever or well-informed, but if Cronus had known about this gate, he wouldn't have let me use it to slip back and forth between Earth and Tartarus all these years, now would he?"

"No, I guess not. I suppose the river monsters discourage anyone from looking for it."

She grins. "Oh, yeah! And that was one of the smaller ones."

I don't even want to think about that. It's not so much that I'm scared as I don't know exactly how much power I have and how quickly I can use it up. I don't want to waste it fighting random monsters. At least that's what I tell myself. The truth is, I'm scared. But not just for myself: for my friends, for my parents, for everyone back on Earth. What my friends and I are doing is important, the most important thing anyone's ever done, and if we screw it up... Well, it won't come to that. It can't.

*We're heroes, right?*

Up ahead, I see an outcropping of rock rising up from the river. That's not unusual, but what's embedded in it is: long white spiky crystals. "Slow down," I tell Charon. "Angle us over to that rock."

"What's up?" Hannah asks.

"Crystals."

"Oh yeah," Mark says. "Good idea! You need to rearm yourself. That was pretty badass the way you shot those crystals from your hand to take out those harpies."

I grin at the memory. "It was, wasn't it? That makeshift armor I made worked out pretty good too. Nessus would have messed me up otherwise."

"It sucks we had to flee," Mark says. "You would have won, I know it."

"The quest is more important," Hannah interrupts. "What use is it to win one battle and lose the war?"

The witch has a point.

Charon brings us to the outcropping and I reach out to grab the crystals. Before I can touch them, they slide out of the rock and fly into my outstretched hands. *OK, that's new, but I like it.* Some of the crystals I grind by squeezing them in my fists. I fuse these to my skin in an effort to repair the cracks in the gemstone and crystal armor covering my chest and shoulders. It was damaged when Nessus stabbed me in our duel, but only because he'd been using one of Ares' magic swords.

"Your wound better?" Mark asks.

I rotate my arm and rub my shoulder. There's a slight twinge, but not much. "I think so... Fast healing is one of the perks of being a Titan."

"You should put that armor all over," he suggests.

"I wish! But nah, man. There aren't enough left to form a complete set of armor, and maybe that's for the best. I'm not sure how wearing a full suit would affect my mobility. Gotta stay fast in a fight."

"Yeah, I get it. Just don't get hit in the back or the side."

"Or anywhere else," Hannah teases.

"Ha, ha. Duly noted." I take the last three spikes and work them one at a time between the knuckles of my right hand. Through my connection to the earth, they slide right in. No blood, no pain. The perfect secret weapon.

"Those ought to come in *handy*," Mark says.

I groan. It's a weak joke, but there's nothing else to laugh at down here, so I give it a few chuckles.

Hannah rolls her eyes. "You about ready, Rock Boy?"

"Almost." I make a fist and will the spikes to reemerge. I hold them up and study them, still not used to my power. With a thought, the spikes retract. "OK," I say. "We can go now."

# 6

LET'S GO SAVE THE WORLD

Our detour stops at a rock wall. A dead end. Mark shouts a warning —a warning I echo—but Charon ignores our increasingly panicked cries.

Hannah doesn't, but reacts with amusement. "Calm down, guys! It's not what you think."

"What do you mean? Tell Charon to stop! We're going to hit the wall—" I brace for impact. Only we don't hit it; we sail right through as if the wall doesn't exist.

"It's an illusion!" Mark says in surprise. "A trick meant to make trespassers turn back."

"Close," Hannah says. "Only it's not an illusion. The wall's real, but not for us—well, not for me, or for Charon." Her raven familiar squawks and she scratches the back of his head. "And not for my precious Shadow. Basically, anyone Hades has granted permission to. And that extends to anyone inside Charon's boat."

I frown. "That's why you're taking us this way, isn't it? Because you don't want us to know about the other back doors? The ones anybody can use?"

"Look, Andrus, I like you, but we only met a few days ago."

I blurt out, "It's because I'm a Titan, isn't it?"

Hannah doesn't answer that. "Maybe this way isn't faster, but it's more secure. If I took you to another gate, one you say 'anybody' can use, what do you think would happen?"

I scowl. "We'd get to the Garden a lot faster!"

"Would we?"

"Well, sure! Except..."

She gives me a pointed look as sharp as any dagger. "Except what?"

"We'd get spotted."

"Not just spotted, genius! We'd be up to our necks in monsters."

"OK," I persist, "but I need you to trust me."

"I do... I trust you to fulfill the quest, but that doesn't mean I trust you with all my secrets, especially the ones that aren't mine to give. I'm loyal to my father, and this is *his* kingdom, not mine."

I nod, not really liking her answer, but understanding it. "So how much further? Another few hours? Because it feels like we've been down here forever."

"Not far," Hannah replies. "Time flows differently in the underworld, slower. Days here equal hours there."

"So we'll come back to Earth soon after we left?" Mark asks.

"Well... It depends on how long this quest takes, but yeah, we shouldn't be gone long."

"So there's still a chance?" Mark asks. "To save my sister? To save Lucy?"

"And my parents?" I add.

Hannah says, "Maybe... The faster we free my father, the better the chance of saving your loved ones."

That seems to satisfy Mark, but I notice Hannah looks away when she says it, and I can't tell if it's because she's hiding something or because she notices the pale gate that glows in the distance.

"Is that it?" Mark asks.

"It sure is," Hannah says. "We made it!"

The gate is ghostly gray, mist-like: a magic portal. Charon steers us through. When we come out, we're in Tartarus. The Kingdom of the Dead at last. It doesn't look like much, just a small damp cove. The skeletal ferryman pulls us alongside an ancient stone dock.

"Thank you," Hannah tells Charon. "My father and I appreciate the risk you're taking on our behalf. Your loyalty will be rewarded."

Charon fixes her with his sightless gaze then bows in a click and clatter of bones.

"Don't worry, old friend. Once my father is free, you'll be back in business ferrying souls in no time."

"Yeah, thanks," I say to Charon. "So are you going to wait here?"

The mummy shakes his head and points back the way we came.

"Why can't he wait?" Mark asks Hannah. "I'd feel safer knowing he's here."

"Someone might get suspicious if he's gone too long from the Styx. This little cove is warded and as "off the grid" as you can get. Besides, I can summon him if we need him again."

"What do you mean 'if'?" I ask.

"We might not be coming back this way. It depends."

"On what?"

"On how successful we are." Hannah climbs out of the boat onto the dock. She walks away as Mark and I look at each other, not sure what to do. When the witch doesn't hear us following, Hannah looks back over her shoulder. "You two coming?"

"Yeah," I say. "In a minute." I turn to Mark and give him a quick pep talk to psych him up, but it's really for both of us. "We got this, man. We're going to march in there and kick some ass!"

"Monster ass?"

"Nah, not just monster ass. All the ass! Now come on, let's go save the world."

When we join Hannah at the far end of the dock, she holds out her hands to stop us from moving forward. "Getting here was the easy part," she warns. "Everything we fought on Earth is nothing compared to what we'll fight here. I want you both to know that, so let it sink in... This is an adventure, but it's dangerous: another world, a world of monsters and magic you can't even begin to imagine! And the stakes—"

"Mark and I know what the stakes are."

She studies my face a moment, then nods. "I guess you do." In a burst of feathers, her familiar launches from her shoulder and goes flapping down the rock passage. "I'm sending Shadow to scout ahead; our telepathic link will warn us of any danger he finds." With that, she swirls her purple cloak around her and resumes walking.

Behind us, Charon guides the boat toward the gate. The living dead man doesn't look back, and neither should I, but I do.

"When we get outside," Hannah says, "we'll be surrounded by ghosts. Act casual. They won't know Mark is alive because of his ghost-mask, and they won't see me at all because my cloak makes me invisible to the dead. I'm too famous and easy to spot otherwise."

"What about me?" I ask. "Won't the ghosts notice I'm alive?"

She snorts. "You're a Titan, remember? You aren't really alive, not in a human sense." When I scowl at her, she quickly adds, "I mean you don't give off 'living' vibes like Mark would. They'll just think you're another ghost unless you do something stupid." She gives me a stern look. "You're not going to, right?"

"No."

"OK, then. Nothing to worry about."

We come to a dead end, but it doesn't stay dead long. There's a secret passage, one Hannah explains only she can open, and when the rock wall slides away, we step out into the Kingdom of the Dead.

# 7

### EVERYTHING'S HUNGRY

THE LANDSCAPE OF TARTARUS VARIES, from jagged, barren rock to lush green valleys of fragrant moss. Gems blanket the cavernous ceiling like stars. Mushrooms carpet the floor. There are bats and rats, owls and ravens, lizards, spiders, and worms—every manner of creeping night-thing. Some are larger than any version on Earth, and we waste precious minutes hiding as a giant centipede crawls by, cruel jaws clicking, antennae waving like whips. Its three hundred legs march the blood-red body along like a hard-shelled army.

"We have to be careful," Hannah warns. "Everything's hungry down here, hungry for one thing or another... Life, death, knowledge, it doesn't matter. Everything wants something, and most are good at getting what they want."

"Are the insects and animals alive?" Mark asks. "Or are they ghosts too?"

"Oh, they're alive. They feed on each other, or the vegetation. And some of them will feed on us if we're not careful."

"Like that centipede?"

"Yep. The bigger they are, the hungrier they get, and they can't eat ghosts."

"Heh! Good point. Which way do we go?"

Hannah scans the horizon, then points toward another river. "That way."

"Is that the Styx again?"

"No, it's the Lethe."

"It looks like the Styx, except the water's green, not black."

"Yeah, well, it isn't."

"What makes it different?" Mark asks.

"This river doesn't go anywhere. Also, it doesn't need monsters. It's its own monster."

"How do you mean?" I ask.

"It's the River of Forgetfulness. Any one, ghost or mortal, who touches it instantly and forever forgets who they are and why they would ever want to leave Tartarus."

I stare at the glittering green water and curse. The Lethe looks wide, and I imagine it's deep—as deep or deeper than the Styx. "What about us? We're not mortal."

"The effect is temporary for us," Hannah says, "but trust me, you don't want to experience it."

"So how do we get across? Call Charon?"

"No, that might draw attention. I've got a better idea. Follow me."

Hannah leads us in the direction the centipede went. Soon, we can see it. Worse, it can see us.

"We're going to ride it," Hannah says.

My jaw drops. "We're going to what?"

"Not ride it exactly; we're going to use it as a boat."

Before I have time to argue, the creature charges, scuttling forward with an angry chittering that sounds like a hundred knives being sharpened.

I draw my sword.

"Don't kill it," Hannah commands. "Distract it."

"How?"

"Run!" Hannah shouts, then flaps her cloak up and turns into a familiar gray fog, a fog that reeks of death. It's what she uses to fly, and she uses her magic now to float up, hovering overhead.

Mark and I don't need to be told twice. We run. The centipede gains. It's not hard; it has three hundred legs and we only have two each.

I dare a backward glance. Hannah materializes on top of the centipede, right behind the bulging, hateful head. She takes out her dagger and does something to the back of the creature's head. She said we weren't going to kill it, so I can't imagine what she's doing.

Whatever she's up to, it works. The centipede slows to a stop twenty feet away. It drools venom, but otherwise makes no aggressive move. Mark and I cautiously approach, each coming around on different sides.

"Come on," Hannah calls. "I promise it won't bite... not unless I tell it to." As if to prove her point, the centipede lowers itself to the cavern floor, making it easy for Mark and I to climb up and join her.

"How did you do it?" I ask.

"Witchcraft." Hannah taps her boot down at the mystic symbol she's scratched into the thing's skull. "It's a symbol of control. It'll do whatever I tell it now."

And it does. She orders it to march us to the river. As we cross the Lethe, Hannah explains there are five rivers in the underworld: some water, some ice, some fire. Ghosts can't travel over water without help, so the outer kingdom is encircled by the River Styx, which is full of monsters. The inner kingdom is encircled by the River Lethe. "Together," she says, "they serve as a double ward against anyone breaking in—or breaking out of Hades' kingdom."

"What about the other rivers?" Mark asks.

"The Acheron is the River of Woe, and it serves to separate the good and peaceable ghost population from the malevolent half."

"You mean Murder Town?"

Hannah nods. "Among others. Only those who truly repent can cross from the evil side to the good, and only those who have given in to cruelty can cross to the evil side. Everyone else is turned back by inconsolable waves of sadness."

"Literal waves?" Mark asks. "Or metaphorical?"

Hannah smirks. "Literal. There are a few exceptions... Those who are morally gray and comfortable with it can freely pass from one side to the other."

"What about the rivers of ice and fire?" I ask.

"Phlegethon is the River of Flame. It leads to the deepest part of Tartarus, to my father's castle and the prison where he kept Cronus and the other Titans. It's also where Cronus rules now." She says this last bit with a grimace.

"And the river of ice?"

"The Cocytus? The River of Wailing is on the deepest level, beneath the castle. That's where Zeus imprisoned the Titans, frozen beneath the ice."

"Do you think that's where Hades is?"

Hannah rolls her eyes. "Too obvious, genius. Guess again."

"But you've checked?" I persist.

"Yes, I've checked. Of course, I have! That was the *first* thing I did, and it was almost the *last*... Cronus hid my father somewhere more clever than that."

"More clever," Mark puts in, "but maybe not more secure?"

Hannah's mood brightens at the suggestion. "I'm beginning to like you, mortal."

Mark frowns. "I thought you already liked me?"

"No, I said I was glad Andrus brought you along. There's a difference."

"Oh," Mark says.

Hannah laughs. Mark looks confused, then he laughs too. I smile, glad to see them getting along, but my mind is already racing ahead, toward the battle I know is coming.

# 8

## THE ASPHODEL MEADOWS

WE LEAVE THE CENTIPEDE BEHIND. Tartarus is big... bigger than I thought. Vast is a better word. And it's gloomy, yet strangely serene and beautiful.

We come into a meadow, filled with strange black flowers and long-stemmed grass. The place has a lazy, untended look. Parts appear to be kept up—the grass cut, the flowers artfully arranged—yet there's no consistency, no pattern. Everywhere I look, I see half-hearted attempts to maintain the work, but no attempt to expand it. Parts are wild, overgrown, encroaching. It's as if whoever's in charge of the project had some grand ambition, then gave up and decided this weird unfinished mess was good enough.

"This is the Asphodel Meadows," Hannah says. "It's where the undistinguished dead live—those who never did anything especially wrong or right in life. It's a boring place, full of boring people. Lots of families, scholars, tradesmen. I never spent much time here. I like to go where the action is."

"Murder Town?" I tease.

She smirks. "Sometimes... Anyway, like I said, these are boring people who don't take risks. That means they'll sell us out to the Titans in a second, so be on your best behavior."

"What's that mean?" I ask.

"I don't know, *act like ghosts.* Be friendly, but don't do anything to stand out. Try not to talk to anyone."

There's a village up ahead, neat rows of white stone houses with blue trim rising up from the meadow. We walk among the ghosts, and the dead carry on with their lives much as I imagined they did in life. Here, they aren't insubstantial. They seem as flesh and blood as any of us, but they don't always stay that way. They can interact with solid objects, but pass through walls like ghosts.

As we continue down the cobblestone street, I notice none of the houses have doors. I guess that's because ghosts don't need them. Still, it makes them seem more like tombs than houses.

"That seems kind of crazy," I whisper to Hannah.

"What?"

"No doors! Anyone could walk into your house any time, any way they want."

"That's not how it works," she replies, then shuts up as a family of ghosts walks by. Father, mother, and two young daughters out for a stroll. Hannah is invisible to them, but the ghosts nod and smile at Mark and me, thinking we're ghosts too. We return the greeting, and the family continues on, chatting about normal things. Well, normal for them. I'm not sure what's normal for me anymore.

Once they're out of earshot, I ask her why.

"Because a house's walls are coded to whoever built it, so only that ghost and the people it gives the code to can come inside."

"Coded?" Mark asks. "You mean like a combination lock?"

"Yes, but it won't work for the living. It's a kind of spiritual lock. See, everything vibrates at a certain frequency, the living, the dead, Earth, Tartarus... It's what keeps our worlds separate. Now ghosts, they operate on a frequency, a frequency that allows them to alter their physical integrity to match whatever object they need to interact with is vibrating at. On Earth, it's not easy, but Tartarus is a different story."

"What's that got to do with locks?" I ask.

Hannah sighs. "I was getting to that. Each ghost invests a certain amount of their spirit into the construction of their home; that causes it to vibrate at a specific frequency customized to them. Kind of like wards, but different. There's also another reason."

"What's that?" Mark asks.

"Having the ghost's home attuned to a specific vibration acts as a kind of portal to Earth."

"You mean to their grave?"

Hannah nods. "Yes, or to wherever they died, or felt most connected to in life. Ghosts are more easily summoned there, more easily communicated with."

"What about your friend, Doctor Herophilos?" I ask. "He didn't die in Bronson Canyon. He died in Ancient Greece, thousands of years ago."

She grins. "I'm a witch, remember? *I know things.* Also, I'm the daughter of Hades. The rules don't apply to me." That ends the conversation.

Mark's stomach growls. When we get to an open air farmer's market, he heads for a fruit vendor's stall. Hannah hisses at him to stop. "You can't eat that!" she warns.

He turns away from the stall, regret in his eyes. "Why not?"

"Because that's *spirit food*, not human food. It nourishes ghosts, but it kills you. Listen to me: You can't eat or drink anything that grows here. If you do, you'll die, and never be able to leave."

Mark blinks at her, then sighs. "But I can't die while Hades is imprisoned."

"That's right, but you can become a zombie. Besides, my dad will be free soon."

His stomach rumbles again. "So what am I supposed to eat?"

Hannah rummages in the leather pouch attached to her belt. She pulls out an energy bar. "Here, eat this."

"What about my ghost-mask? Won't I have to take it off first?"

"No. The mask is made of magic vapor. You can pass harmless things through it, like food and water—as long as it's from Earth."

"Oh," Mark says. "That's pretty cool. I was worried I'd have to do this quest on an empty stomach."

"Nope," she says. "See? I thought of everything."

My stomach rumbles too. I shoot the witch an awkward grin.

"Really?" Hannah says. "You too?"

I shrug. "What can I say? Saving the world makes me hungry."

"Fine." She hands me an energy bar, then opens a third one for herself, nibbling on it and feeding some to Shadow.

"This whole place is deadly," Mark grumbles.

Hannah rolls her eyes. "Not if you're a ghost."

"No," he says, "I suppose not. But it's not exactly paradise either."

"There are places like that," Hannah says. "Beautiful, heavenly places: Elysium, and beyond that, the Fortunate Isles. But they're reserved for heroes, and for those who achieved greatness in life: feats of knowledge, virtue, sacrifice, that sort of thing."

"Can we visit those places?" Mark asks.

Hannah shakes her head. "They're not on our way. Maybe, when this is all over, I'll take you there."

"I want to go there when I die." Mark's voice is full of determination. "I don't want to end up here, trapped with the undistinguished dead. I don't want to be a Loser in the afterlife too!"

"You won't," I tell him, but he gives me a troubled look. I realize he's worried he'll end up here, trapped for all eternity with his drunk mother, trading one life of poverty for another, only this one would stretch on forever...

"And Lucy?" Mark asks. "What about her? She sacrificed herself so we could escape."

"Hey, man! Come on, she's going to be fine." I put a hand on his shoulder, but he shrugs it off.

"You don't know that!"

It's true. I don't, but I have to hope, have to believe Lucy's going to be all right. If she isn't... Hannah mentioned sacrifice was one way to get into paradise. *But there's a difference between sacrifice and revenge.*

When Lucy attacked Inquisitor Anton—when she buried her knife in his chest—how much of that was for us, and how much was for her? And does that make a difference in the afterlife? Should it?

Or does only the end result matter? I don't know, and I know better than to bring it up now.

We walk on, each of us together, yet alone. We walk through ghost-traveled streets, and it's almost normal. Almost home. It makes me miss Othrys. It makes me miss my life, my family, my Lucy... But that's why we're here. That's why we're fighting—and that's why we'll win.

# 9

## THE GARDEN OF BONE

WE SOON LEARN why it's called the Garden of Bone. There are bones growing out of the ground. Giant bones: rib cages and skulls, mostly. I don't have time to ask whether they're really growing there or were placed on purpose, and I suppose it doesn't matter. What matters is there are a lot of monsters camped here; some I'm familiar with, like centaurs and harpies, and one I'm not: cyclopes. These one-eyed giants lumber along, guarding the perimeter. They're brutish, tusked like wild boars, and wear sheepskin loincloths. Their hands carry clubs and axes, simple weapons for simple smashing. Each cyclops stands twenty feet tall and looks twice as mean.

Towering above them all is the Lesser Titan called Gyges, as tall as the rock climbing wall in the Harryhausen Gym back home. He has fifty heads and a hundred arms, each uglier than the last. Not all the heads are human, or even human-ish. Some are reptilian, some bird-like, some insect, while others are bestial: lions, bears, wolves. *Drooling, screeching, growling.* They glare out in every possible direction. Likewise, not all the giant's arms are human-like either. Some are tentacles, and still others are the pincers of crabs.

The worst part is the central "face" in Gyges' torso. The best I can do is describe it as some sort of spider-thing, with eight jet-black eyes surrounding the fanged and suckered mouth of a lamprey or leech. Beneath that terrible visage, the lower-half descends into the dark-furred haunches of a goat, yet the black taloned feet are those of a great eagle. The combination is so horrible, yet so fascinating, it's hard to look away.

In the center of the camp is a prison cell literally made from the ribcage of some monster. And inside that cage is a huge three-headed dog: Cerberus. The red-eyed beast howls for its lost master, an unearthly sound. There's an almost human quality to it, an emotional depth that's anguish beyond animal. But there's a monstrous quality too, like a pack of wolves sharing the same body, which of course is what Cerberus is. The creature raises one lonesome head at a time, each separate howl rising to join the previous until they become a single midnight chorus, then veering off into their own song. Three voices, one body. It's an eerie effect, and it would be bone-chilling if I hadn't seen Gyges first or known Cerberus was going to be on our side.

We're hiding behind a boulder a half-mile away from the Garden, at the edge of a forest of enormous mushrooms, their stems as thick as tree trunks, their white caps as wide as tents.

"You didn't tell us Gyges was going to be that ugly." I say in half-jest, half-horror. "How the hell is that thing even alive?"

Hannah shrugs. "The same way you're alive: *magic*. And just like you, Gyges shouldn't be alive, but there he is. Think you can take him?"

"Take him? Are you kidding? He's fifty feet tall!"

"Yeah," she agrees. "It's a problem."

"What about your magic dagger?" Mark asks her.

"What about it?"

"You used it to control the centipede. Couldn't you fly over and use it on Gyges?"

I clap Mark on the back. "Good thinking! If Hannah can mind control him, we could take out those monsters easy."

"I'd love to," Hannah says, though I'm not sure how much of that is sarcasm. "Except my dagger doesn't work on Titans—even lesser ones like giants. Besides, even if it did, it's only meant to control one brain, not fifty."

I frown. "Fifty brains? Gyges doesn't look that smart."

"Trust me," Hannah says, "the giant's no genius, but he's not stupid, either. Don't underestimate him. And not to lecture, but just because something's ugly, doesn't mean it's not smart. Look at Medusa."

"I'd rather not."

"Ha, ha," the witch mock-laughs. "You know you're related to Gyges, right?"

"I guess it's like Captain Nessus," I say. "We underestimated him, and look what happened."

"Actually," Mark says, "*you* underestimated him. I hid in the alley."

"I remember. Let's not make the same mistake twice."

We duck behind the boulder to think. It bothers me a little, what Hannah said, about me being related to Gyges. It's true, which doesn't make it any easier, but it's something I'll have to get used to. Maybe I can find a way to use it to my advantage...

When nothing comes to mind, I ask, "Didn't you and Ares have a plan?"

"Sure," she says, "to get you down here."

"And after that?"

Hannah shrugs. "We figured things would sort themselves out."

"But you didn't count on Gyges."

"We didn't count on a lot of things, Andrus! How could we?"

"I don't know, maybe because you're Gods?"

"I'm a Demigoddess," Hanna corrects me, "and Ares is an avatar, so he's only one aspect of himself, a fraction of his power."

"Where's the rest of him?" Mark asks.

Again, Hannah shrugs. "During the Gods War, several of the Gods split themselves into multiple avatars to carry the fight to Earth, each focusing on a different aspect of the war. Some of those Gods were killed."

"And their avatars?"

"The avatars are all that's left. They're divine essences trapped in mortal shells. Most were hunted down by the NGT and destroyed before Hades was captured. Ares is the only one left, at least the only one I've been able to find."

"What happens to Ares if his host body is damaged or destroyed?" Mark asks.

"Without his God body to return to, his essence would have no place to go. He'd be lost, doomed, and slowly fade away."

"Oh," Mark says, then manages the courage to peer over the boulder again. "What if Ares found another host?"

"The host would have to be willing, and would have to be magically prepared to receive him."

"Could Ares go into one of you?"

"No, because Andrus and I have our own essences that block possession. There's no room for others to come in."

"I see," Mark says. "What about me?"

"What about you what?"

"Could Ares come into me? Could I be his avatar?"

"Sure," Hannah says, "but Ares' current avatar would have to be close, and so far as we know, he's still back on Earth."

"What if he was here?" Mark asks. "Like how close would he have to be?"

"The closer, the better."

"What about a half-mile? Would that be close enough?"

Hannah and I look at each other, each getting the same idea, so when we join Mark in peering over the boulder, we're not surprised to see we're right. We know why Mark is asking all these questions: *The Garden of Bone is getting a new arrival.*

Captain Nessus, my old enemy, gallops in ahead of his Night Patrol. He's a centaur: part-man, part-horse, part-ram. His shaggy face is gray, wild-maned, with glaring yellow eyes, sharp teeth, and long, curling horns set atop a high, hard-ridged forehead.

He brings with him a company of centaurs, including his brothers, Democ and Ruvo. The centaurs carry long barbed harpoons in their clawed hands; each weapon tethered by a rope to their utility belts. A centaur's favorite trick is to stick their harpoon in you, then break into a gallop, dragging you behind them. But they're famous for something far worse, and that's grabbing their victims by their necks, lifting them up to watch them strangle, then head-butting them to crack open the skull. Then they eat your brain...

Above the centaurs, a flock of harpies fly. They're black-feathered scavengers: half-woman, half-vulture, with razor-sharp beaks and talons.

But it's not the centaurs and harpies that draw my attention. It's the prisoner in the bone cage-cart they've brought with them: *Mr. Cross.* Our gym teacher is Ares' current avatar. He'd had to blow his cover to save us back on Earth, and the last we'd seen, he'd been holding off Captain Nessus and the Night Patrol. That had bought us enough time to make it through the gate to the Underworld. Hard to believe that was yesterday...

Yesterday, when we were on Earth. Yesterday, when everything had seemed so full of hope. Hope that turned to horror. Horror that turned into this mad quest. I'd lost confidence when I'd seen Gyges, but now, maybe, with Mr. Cross we have a chance.

"They're going to imprison him," I say. "Do we free him, or do this ritual to make Mark his new avatar?"

"Hang on." Hannah sends Shadow to scout out the situation. As she does, her eyes roll back in her head and her body goes still. She's seeing through her familiar now, getting a real "bird's-eye" view.

"You sure you know what you're asking, Mark?"

"Well, no. Not a hundred-percent. All I know is I'm not much use in a fight, and Mr. Cross—I mean, Ares—is. I could be a lot more helpful if I was Ares."

"You're plenty helpful now," I tell him. "Don't be so down on yourself. Pretty much all the best ideas we've had have come from you. We'll lose that if you become Ares' avatar."

He shrugs. "But you'll gain another fighter. *A powerful one.* Brains can only get us so far with what we're up against. There's no way we're going to be able to sneak a three-headed dog out of the enemy camp. And I'm not sure we can even free Mr. Cross. Better to have Ares out here with us when we go in."

Mark makes a good point, but it's not one I'm ready to concede. "I don't know if it's going to come to that. Hannah's got her cloak; she can just mist out and sneak in. She could probably free Ares that way."

"Maybe," Mark concedes, "and I know it's blasphemy, but I always wanted to be a God... or a Titan."

I shake my head. "Trust me, it's not that great. At least you know what you are."

"Yeah, that's the problem. I'm only human. If I wasn't... if I wasn't maybe I could have done something back at the gym. I could have stopped Anton. I could have saved Lucy!"

"Hey, you don't know that. It all happened too fast. There was nothing anyone could do." I say the words, but as I do, I wonder. *Is there something different I could have done?* If I'd known what I am, if I'd understood my powers better, maybe... maybe things didn't have to play out the way they did. But I see Anton's mace swing. I see it swing and come down on Lucy's head. I hear the sound, the sound no one should hear. And I see Lucy fall.

I shut my eyes against the pain. Against the memory burned into my brain. I replace it with another memory, a sweeter one...

To the night I first met Mark's sister, to how Lucy and I had stayed up late together. We'd talked, and done more than talked. I remember her telling me how she'd done so much to save her brother's academic career by sacrificing her own. 'I'm no hero,' she'd told me. 'I just did what I had to do.'

And I'd told her, "I've been thinking maybe being a hero isn't about saving the world. Maybe it's about the small stuff, saving one person at a time. Including yourself.'

Lucy had come into my arms then. Eyes wet, lips trembling. We'd kissed. There was heat in it, passion, and we'd let it linger. When it was over, Lucy said, 'That was nice, but it doesn't have to mean anything.'

But it did mean something. We tried to fight it, but the attraction was too strong. And when she'd ended up in my bed, I remember that night too...

I remember Lucy's smile in the darkness, remember her reaching down and pulling my hand to her face. She'd planted a kiss on my palm, then pressed my hand to her cheek. 'I wanted to be with you tonight,' she'd said, 'because tomorrow... well, we don't know what's going to happen. I don't want to have any regrets.'

'Yeah,' I'd said. 'I don't want any either...'

Only that's as far as it had gone. And I did have regrets. Regrets we hadn't made love, regrets I hadn't been able to save her, and I wonder if things had been different... Well, I wonder a lot of things.

"Hey," Mark says, "Andrus, you all right?"

I open my eyes and let go of the past. It can't help me now. I don't know what can.

"What's wrong?" Mark asks.

"Nothing, man. I was just... Don't worry about it. Why, what's up?"

"I wanted to ask you something before Hannah gets back."

I look at the witch, but she's still frozen in place, eyes pure white. "What is it?"

"If I... If I become Ares' avatar, it's like being possessed. I'll still be in there, but deep down, buried. I'm not sure how much I'll be aware of what's going on."

"Yeah, so?"

"Well..." Mark's eyes dart from me to Hannah and back again. "I might not want to stay possessed forever. And if anything were to happen..."

"Like what?"

Mark shrugs. "Like anything, I don't know. We just met Hannah and Ares and they saved us, but I'm not sure how much I trust them. I mean, I trust them, but not necessarily in everything, you know? She wouldn't even tell us how to escape Tartarus without her."

"I noticed."

"Exactly," Mark says. "Maybe it means something, maybe it doesn't. All I know is the Gods and Titans have a long history of hatred and betrayal, and I don't want to end up on the wrong side if things go south."

The truth is, I'm glad Mark is being cautious, glad he shares a little of my paranoia, but I don't want to tell him I'm worried because I don't want to worry him. I also don't want to believe it's true. "So what are you saying?" I ask.

"I'm saying, I trust *you*, Andrus. I was raised to be a priest of the Titans, not the Gods. And just because things haven't worked out with Cronus, doesn't mean things have to work out bad with all the Titans."

"You mean like Prometheus? The Titan who helped humanity before the Gods War? Fat lot of good it did him!" I remember his story, how he'd been the most clever Titan, a trickster yet a diplomat. He'd stayed out of the first war between the Gods and the Titans, playing one side against the other, somehow coming out smelling like a rose in the end. He'd been one of the few Titans Zeus hadn't punished, but the Sky God's mercy hadn't lasted long.

Prometheus had stolen sacred fire from Mount Olympus, and that was bad enough, but he had given it to mortals, and no amount of raging by the Gods could take it back. That fire changed the course of humanity, from being at the mercy of the Gods to striving to become them. Ambition, industry, everything had come out of that gift. It had been the beginning of the end for the Gods, a slow decline into obscurity and spiritual disrepute. And it laid the foundation for the Titans to be freed from their icy prison. Prometheus must have known that, and revenge, rather than altruism, must have been his motive.

Regardless of why he did it, Zeus had punished the rogue Titan, chaining him to a rock and setting a giant eagle upon him. An eagle that ripped out and ate his organs every day, only for them to grow back. No one knew where the rock was, and no one cared.

Prometheus was forgotten, nor did his brothers and sisters come looking for him after their release. They blamed the renegade Titan for not siding with them during the first war, so they wanted no part of him in the second. 'Let him rot,' seemed to be the general consensus, at least so far as the NGT preached.

For all I know, Prometheus is still out there, still chained, still tortured. It's a lesson, a harsh one, and makes me wary of siding with Gods, even ones I know. Sure the circumstances are different, but who knows what could happen after we win? I just have to tell myself Hades is not Zeus, and I am not Prometheus.

Everything's going to work out and be "happily ever after" except that's how fairy tales end. Not myths and legends.

"No, man," Mark says. "Not Prometheus! What he did is great and all, but he's old news. I'm talking about you. I could be a priest of *you*."

I start to laugh, but when I see the sincerity in his eyes, the faith, it stops me cold. "We're friends," I say. "That's all I need you to be."

"Still," Mark says. "I think we need a code word."

"A code word?"

"Yeah. Something you wouldn't accidentally say. Something that I might hear when I'm possessed, and know that means you need me to force Ares out."

"You can do that?"

He nods. "Possession has to be willing or it doesn't work. So unless I hear you say the word, I'll know it's safe to stay possessed."

"OK, but I'm not sure we're going to need it."

"Neither am I, but just in case. You brought me along for my brain, remember? And this might be the last time I get to use it."

"So what's the code word?"

Mark thinks a minute. "*Aristea*. It's the Greek word for 'day of glory,' and it's tied to the legend of King Agamemnon, who led his army to triumph over Troy, only to be betrayed by his friends and allies. And there's another reason. Agamemnon was the only hero in the Trojan War who never needed or asked for help from the Gods."

"I remember."

Mark raises an eyebrow. "You do?"

"I didn't sleep through all of Mrs. Ploddin's history lessons. If it was about war or fighting, I paid attention. But all that other stuff, who married who, and who wrote this or that, it just didn't hold my interest."

"And you're paying attention now?"

"Sure."

"Then say the code word."

"Aw, come on, man..."

"This is important! Say it."

I feel foolish, but say the word, "Aristea," then repeat it.

Mark nods. "OK, thanks. Don't use it unless you need to."

"I won't."

"Won't what?" Hannah asks.

We both turn to stare at her as she comes out of her trance. "Nothing," I say. "I was just wondering if I should wake you because you were taking so long, but Mark talked me out of it."

Hannah stretches and yawns as her eyes roll back to normal. "Good. It's bad luck to disturb a witch from her trance."

"So what'd you see?" I ask.

"They've broken Ares' vessel," Hannah says, then when she can tell we don't know what she means, adds, "His arms, his legs, his ribs. They're arguing about how they're going to eat him. *Alive.* Captain Nessus wants the brain, Gyges wants the divine essence, and the harpies... well, they want the eyes and... the parts that make him a man."

I make a face that looks how my stomach feels. "Not sure we needed all those details."

"I didn't tell you what the cyclopes want... Anyway, they hadn't figured out the best way for everyone to get what they want—it's not every day you get to eat an avatar, and there's some concern about whether Ares might taste better pre- or post-essence. I left Shadow to keep an eye on things. He'll let me know if the monsters come to an agreement on the menu."

"Shouldn't we go in now, while they're distracted?" I ask.

"Never get between a monster and its meal," Hannah says. "I'm sorry about Mr. Cross, but he's not getting out of this. Ares still can, if Mark becomes his new avatar."

"So let's do it," Mark says.

And we do.

# 10

---

THE RITUAL

THE RITUAL INVOLVES STRIPPING Mark down to his shorts while Hannah paints his body in mystic symbols. She's chanting the whole time and asked me not to interrupt her, so all I can do is play lookout. I hope Hannah knows what she's doing. I hope Mark does too.

I wonder what Mr. Cross is like—the real Mr. Cross, a man I never knew, but only thought I did. He was always Ares, God of War.

I know Ares must want this ritual, but I wish I knew Mr. Cross wanted it too. But he'd agreed to let Ares in, to become his avatar, so he must have known this day would come... Although I'm sure he envisioned a more glorious death, not being eaten by monsters. That must be horrible! But maybe Mr. Cross is buried down so deep he doesn't know what's going on. Maybe he won't feel anything... at least, not until after we remove Ares' essence and end the possession. Then he'll know. Then he'll know and worse than know, he'll *feel* every inch of those fangs and claws ripping into him...

Should I save him? That's not really the question, though it's a good one. Of course I should. The real question is, *can I?* The answer is no. I can't save anyone, not even myself, not until after we free Hades. Then everything changes.

Anyway, after this is all over, I'll petition Hades to let Mr. Cross live in Elysium, or the Fortunate Isles, someplace nice. A place for heroes. I hope I won't have to petition for anyone else. Mom, Dad... Lucy... even Mark. I feel so powerless! And that's the worst kind of pain, especially when you're like me and you have all these abilities, all this magic, and it's still not enough.

It's never enough.

There's always someone stronger. Someone who wants what you have, or wants to prevent you from having what they have. Even when it's in their best interest to share. If Ouranos, the Sky-Father, hadn't been jealous of his children with Gaia, the Earth-Mother, then the Titans wouldn't have rebelled. And if Cronus hadn't worried that his children would usurp him, then the Gods War would never have happened—not the first, nor the last. None of this would have happened, and a lot more people would be alive, and me... Well, I wouldn't be a Titan, would I?

No, I'd still be a rock. A damned rock!

So as much as I hate everything that's happened, I can't hate it all. Not completely, or I'd have to hate myself. The Gods War made me. All I can do is learn the lessons Ouranos and Cronus never learned, and the lesson Zeus should have: *When you have the chance to kill your enemies, you kill them.* You don't imprison them in ice in another dimension because someday, they're going to get out. Everything bad thing gets out sooner or later. Maybe that's the way it's supposed to be, because once evil rises, good rises too.

And I am good.

I have to be, but I'm a Titan too... Like Gyges, but not like him, and not like Cronus. I imagine myself to be more like Prometheus, friend to man, God, and Titan alike. That's the kind of Titan I want to be. Otherwise, what's the point? There's enough evil in the world without adding mine to it. Yet I wonder... What if I absorbed not just some of Cronus's power, but some of his evil as well? I can't think about that. Not now, not ever.

I shake my head to clear it. Hannah is still muttering her incantations over Mark. *Time to get back to work. Guard duty...*

In the Garden of Bone, the monsters are still there, still arguing, though there's cruel laughter peppered between the hard words.

I remember when I tried to win an argument with Captain Nessus after Mark and I were caught breaking curfew last week. It didn't go well. Monsters enjoy arguing even more than people. It's another kind of hunt to them, stalking prey with words, seasoning meat with the juices of fear...

I sneak a glance at Hannah, so intent on her witchcraft. Mark is out of it now, in some kind of trance. He must really be deep. Hannah's chant rises, a language even older than Greek. Mark's chest heaves, his spine arches, and his eyes snap open. First white, then glowing gold, then blood-red. The glow holds like that, then the unnatural color fades. Mark's body goes limp and his eyes shut.

"Is he OK?" I ask Hannah. "Is it done?"

She brushes strands of black hair from her face and wipes the sweat from her brow. "Your friend is fine," she says, panting. "It's Ares we need to be concerned about."

"Why? Didn't the ritual work?"

She doesn't answer, just breathes heavily.

"Hannah?"

"Just... Look, we'll know in a minute. Sorry, a ritual of this magnitude takes a lot out of me."

"But you did it, right?"

Hannah gives a weary nod, then collapses, back pressed to the boulder. "Yeah, I did it." She reaches into her belt pouch and pulls out a vial, some kind of magic potion—or alcohol, I'm not sure which. She uncorks it and pours the liquid down her throat. When she sees me staring at her, she downs the last of it, then wipes her wrist across her lips. "Don't judge. It's to help me recover."

"I don't care about that. What about Mark? Does he need some? Do you have more?"

"No."

"But look at him! He's not moving."

"That's normal."

"Normal? You call that 'normal'? Nothing's normal anymore!"

Hannah sighs. "Nothing ever was. You just didn't know it until now."

I open my mouth to say something, but she's right of course. Up until a few days ago, my life has been a beautiful lie, a sheltering cocoon. Now the truth is out, and it's eating me alive.

"Look, I get it. It's a lot. But it's real, and it's happening."

"And us?"

Hannah shrugs. "We just have to roll with the punches, that's all."

"No, I don't mean that. I don't mean the ritual or the quest, or..." I wave my hand around to indicate Tartarus. "I mean, *us*."

"What about us?"

"Are we cool?"

"What, you mean me and you?"

"Yeah."

"We're fine, cool, whatever."

"OK, but are we friends?"

She frowns. "Andrus, there's something you should know about me. I don't... I don't make friends easily. When you're hunted by Cronus, it's hard to make friends, even harder to keep them. Things happen to the people I care about. *Bad things*."

"And you think something bad going to happen to me?"

Hannah's eyes narrow, then she snorts and looks away. "Only if you let it."

"I don't mean an accident or losing in battle. Do you think I could turn bad? Evil? Because of my father?" *My real father*, I remind myself. *Cronus*.

She shrugs. "I don't know. We're all shadows of our parents: their hopes and dreams as much as their hates and fears. It's up to us what we do with them."

"Yeah, I get that, but Cronus is evil, so I feel like I'm starting at a disadvantage."

A long sigh escapes her. "Andrus, even Cronus didn't start life evil. He may have had inclinations, but he didn't have to make the choices he did. OK, maybe some of them... His own father, Ouranos, wanted him dead, and to murder all his brothers and sisters too. So Cronus made hard choices, and if he'd stopped there, maybe he would have been all right. But he didn't. He just kept making hard choices until they were easy, and better than easy. He made them until he liked them, and then they weren't choices anymore, because he was always going to pick the wrong one, the evil one. And who knows? To Cronus, the things he does make sense. They must, but only *to him*. He's protecting himself, his empire, his brothers and sisters. Avenging them. But to everyone else, he's a monster."

"Like those things in the Garden?"

"No, not like them. Harpies and centaurs may be nasty, but they're monsters with a small 'm.' Cronus is a Monster with a capital 'M,' and he's got to be stopped! It's up to us to stop him."

"By freeing your father."

"Yes. Hades will fix everything. He has to. I know he will. I know it..." The strain in her voice is obvious, the tears in her eyes are real. This is what Hannah's been fighting for her whole life. All these years, she's been racing toward her destiny, while I've been running from mine.

I give her a minute, then ask, "What happens after?"

She looks up, confused. "What do you mean? The world gets set right."

"I don't mean the world."

"You mean to you?"

"Yes, to me."

She shrugs. "Not my decision."

"But if it was?"

She smiles. "Seriously? Relax."

"Tell me."

"Ok, fine... I'd keep you around. Probably."

"Why probably?"

"Because you might do something to piss me off between now and then." She ratchets her smile up a notch, turns it into a playful grin.

I try to read past the expression, past the even white teeth and flashing dark eyes. Does Hannah mean it? I'm not sure. She sounds sincere, as sincere as any witch I've ever heard—the only one.

Behind her, Mark stirs. Or rather, something inside him stirs. Under the skin. Stretching it.

"What is it?" I cry in alarm, going to Mark's side. "What have you done to him?"

"It's Ares settling in. It's normal... I think."

"You think? I thought you'd done this ritual before?"

"I never said that."

"Mark?" I say, shaking him. "Wake up, Mark!"

"I wouldn't do that," Hannah warns.

"Why not?"

Mark's hands shoot up and grab my wrists, and in a voice that's deep and his yet not his, he growls, "Because I don't like it."

# 11

## A WEAPON AS SHARP AS ANY

"Ares? Is that you?" I ask.

"It is." The God of War releases his grip on my wrist and sits up slowly, grunting. "*Ugh!* You two did well to get me out of that last vessel."

"Mark helped."

Ares looks down at his skinny new teenage body. "So he did. Although this vessel is not one I would have chosen, it is appreciated nonetheless—as is his sacrifice." The God gets up and stretches, joints popping. Settling into his new skin.

"Can Mark still hear me?" I ask. "Does he know what's going on?"

"Your friend is safe," Ares replies. "There are few places safer than inside a God, even a God of War."

"But is he aware?" I persist.

Ares shrugs. "To a limited degree. I can call him forth if you wish to ascertain he is well."

"Would you?"

Ares looks from me to Hannah, who nods. "Very well, but only for a moment. It is unwise to interfere with my control, especially this early in the process." The God's body goes stiff, his eyes roll up, and when they roll back down, the gaze *feels* different, the posture shifts from ramrod straight to Mark's comfortable slouch.

"Mark?"

"Yeah, man. It's me."

"You OK?"

He nods. "It's weird! Not bad, though. Like being asleep..."

"Can you hear what's going on? Can you see through your eyes? You know, when Ares in control?"

"A little, not much."

"See?" Hannah says. "Didn't I tell you? Everything's fine."

"Ares wants to come back now," Mark says. His eyes start to roll back, his body tense.

"Wait!" I shout.

Mark's eyes snap back, then start going all dreamy.

"Thanks, buddy. Thanks for this."

Mark smiles, then his face goes slack. The eyes do their thing again, and then it's Ares standing before me. "I trust you are satisfied?"

"Yeah."

"I know it's hard," Hannah says, "but Mark is safer now. He can defend himself, and more than that, he can be useful in a fight. We needed his brains before, but now... well, we need the God of War."

There's no arguing with that. "What about Mr. Cross?" I ask. "Isn't there anything we can do for him?"

As if on cue, my gym teacher's screams echo across the field.

"To cease his agony, we must free Hades."

"But isn't there something we can do now?"

"No, Andrus. To charge into battle without a plan might win us glory, but it will not save your teacher, nor will it further our cause. There is too much at stake. Far too much, but rest assured, those creatures will pay."

"So I assume we're going to sneak into the Garden, that's one problem, but how are we going to get away? Cerberus is as big as a truck! How are we supposed to sneak him out, much less travel with him? We'll draw too much attention! The monsters can follow us easily. Even if we give them the slip through magic or whatever, it's not like they won't know where we're going. All they have to do is head us off at Hades' prison."

Ares nods in approval. "You make good points, Titan. Brute force cannot win this battle, nor can pure stealth. A different strategy is called for."

"Like what? Diplomacy?"

Ares laughs. "No, though words are a weapon as sharp as any—or so my brother, Apollo, always insisted. Of course, he's dead, so maybe his advice wasn't the best. Sometimes the sharpest weapon is still a sword—it's certainly the quickest, and the most certain."

"I think you're right. So are you going to tell me what this strategy is?"

The War God shakes his head. "No, Andrus, I'm waiting for you to tell me."

"Me? But you're the expert!"

"I am, but I'm also curious to see if you have your father's devious mind. Think, Andrus! *Strategize.*"

"You're wasting time! We could be going down there, we could be saving Mr. Cross..."

"No, *you're* wasting time. Think!"

"Do it," Hannah says. "I know it doesn't seem important, but it is."

"Oh, it seems important, but I don't get why you're leaving it up to me."

Hannah rests a hand on my shoulder. "Think."

I wrack my brain, fighting past the anger, the desperation, the fear. What if I get it wrong? A God will laugh at me. Hannah will laugh at me. What if I come up with something that sounds good, but gets us all captured? Or worse? What if my next thoughts blow the whole quest?

"Ares said to think," Hannah says, "not overthink."

"I'm trying."

"Try harder. If you were Cronus, what would you do?"

"But I'm not! Why would you even ask that?"

Hannah exchanges a look with Ares. "Forget it. Let's not push it."

"Hannah? What is this? What are you and Ares up to?"

She turns around and slaps me. Hard. My anger flares, but that's the end of her violence. She doesn't even seem upset. She just steps back, a curious look on her face. It's similar to the look Ares has. It infuriates me, like I'm some kind of science project.

My rage builds, molten-hot, and I feel myself losing control... losing myself into something bigger than me. Something older and infinitely more powerful. I hear the voice of Cronus... no, not the voice, the thoughts. Only they are my thoughts. Jumbled, broken, yet growing clearer. If I can just focus...

*If I can just think!*

There's a darkness looming, pitch-black. Eternal. The kind that can cover the world. My world. My mind. I fall into it, a vast sea of nothing.

# 12

## SOMEONE ELSE'S DREAM

ANOTHER SLAP JOLTS ME out of my trance. I open my eyes. For a moment, I feel myself far away—in Cronus, *as* Cronus. And then I'm not. I'm just me. I'm on the ground. Hannah's on top, hand raised, ready to give me another slap.

"I'm up," I mumble. There's still strong emotion flowing through me, but now it's not hate, it's confused. I'm not sure what it is... I look at Hannah, feel her on top of me, and then I'm not confused anymore. I know exactly what I'm feeling, and she does too.

The witch gets off me in a hurry. "You're up, all right."

I sit up, feeling weird and more than a little embarrassed. "Um, so I had this dream..."

She rolls her eyes. "I'll bet! See, Ares? I told you it wouldn't work. Andrus just isn't strong enough."

Ares steps forward. "Let's not be hasty. Go on, Andrus, tell me about your dream."

I rub my forehead, running my fingers through my hair. "It was... it was like I was Cronus, like I was inside him..." I don't mention it felt strangely safe and familiar.

Ares smiles. "Go on."

"We had this connection, and..."

Ares kneels beside me. "And what?"

I feel the answer on the tip of my tongue, but then a darkness settles in and it starts to slip away. I chase after it in my mind. I chase after it and grab it, rend it, tear it wide open. "I've got it," I say. "I know what we need to do."

"Good!" Ares says, clapping me on the shoulder. "Good, Andrus! I knew you could do it."

"What did I do?"

"First, tell us what you saw in Cronus' mind. Then the answers."

"All right. It's hard to describe, like I was in someone else's dream. A dream I could shape..."

Ares' smile widens and even Hannah seems interested now.

"So what I saw was... Cronus wants Cerberus kept out in the open like this."

"As a show of strength," Ares says. "He wants the symbol of Hades' power on display as his prisoner, and a warning to anyone who might resist."

"That, and also as a trap. The Garden of Bone is well-defended, sure, but why assign only one Lesser Titan to the job?"

"Gyges' brothers are guarding the main gate," Hannah says. "I've seen them there."

"Yes, but there are plenty of other Lesser Titans who could join him. Or why not assign one of the Major Titans?"

"They're not great at taking orders," Hannah says. "That's one of the reasons they lost to the Gods in the past."

"Actually," Ares adds, "we aren't that great at it either. Obedience to others isn't high on any God's priority list, or any Titans'. When you have our kind of power, it takes a lot to bring us together, and even more to hold us there."

"The Gods are better at it than the Titans," Hannah says haughtily. "We Olympians are a tighter knit family."

Ares snorts. "I suppose, at least for the first generation like Zeus and your father. Spending time imprisoned in Cronus' stomach must be good for family bonding... but you know that, don't you, Andrus?"

He says it without malice, so I don't take offense. "Actually, I was alone back then, or not alive enough to know if I wasn't... Anyway, back to what I was saying: The Garden of Bone is a trap."

"You mean besides the obvious horde of monsters?" Hannah asks.

"Yeah, because that's not really Cerberus."

Hannah does a double-take. "It's not? What is it then?"

"An illusion."

Hannah curses and stomps her foot. "What the hell? We went to a lot of trouble to get here, and now you tell me it was all for nothing?"

"Not for nothing. When I was inside Cronus' mind, I saw where the real Cerberus is being kept."

"I knew it!" Ares says. "I knew you could do it, Andrus. So where is he?"

"Not far," I say with a grin.

"This is no time for fooling around," the witch complains.

"So who's fooling? He's underneath the cage with the illusion, in some kind of stone cell, though I suppose you could call it a tomb. And he's alive, in some kind of magic stasis so he doesn't need air—or whatever passes for it in Tartarus."

"So tell us how we get to him," Ares says, and I can tell it's not a question. He actually expects me to know the answer.

"Well?" Hannah demands.

"Give him a moment," Ares says.

"Look, I appreciate the vote of confidence, but I really don't..." I stop before I finish the sentence, because I realize that's not true. I do know how to free Cerberus, I'm just not sure I can.

# 13

---

BELIEVE

My plan is to use my earth magic to tunnel to Cerberus and sneak him out that way. The only problem is I've never used my powers to dig a tunnel before. Sure, I've caved some in, but that was quick and easy. Digging requires a sustained effort.

"You're the son of Cronus and Gaia," Ares reminds me, "the two most powerful wielders of earth magic. Of course you can do it."

"It's a good plan," Hannah says. "Mark would be proud."

I shrug off the compliment. "What if something goes wrong? What if I can't do it?"

"*Believe,*" Ares says. "Believe in yourself. Believe in your power! That's half the battle, right there."

"And the other half?"

Hannah steps in. "Getting others to believe in your power. It's a God thing... and a Titan thing."

"Makes sense. Doesn't make me feel any better, but it makes sense."

"You can do this, Andrus," Hannah says.

"Is that why you slapped me? To get me angry? To get me to tap into my rage? Is that how I was able to get into Cronus' mind?"

Hannah nods. "Ares and I weren't sure you could do it, but we had to try. If we'd warned you ahead of time, you might have resisted. You might have overthought it or doubted your ability, or just plain tried too hard. Any one of those would have prevented you from establishing the telepathic connection, and we don't have time for that."

I scowl at them both. "We need to trust each other, and secrets don't help."

"Except when they do," Ares says. "This one did."

As much as I want to be mad at them, they're right. I can sense it. "OK, but no more surprises. I expect them from our enemies, I don't want to worry about my friends too."

"I can't promise not to slap you," Hannah says, "but if I do, it won't be part of some secret plan."

"No? Then what will it be for?"

She grins. "Because you deserve it."

I feel myself blush and quickly look away, toward the Garden of Bone. "Um, so yeah... I'm gonna have to try and do this tunnel thing from here since we can't get any closer without being spotted. Should you guys come with me or hang back here in case something goes wrong?"

"Cerberus knows us," Hannah says.

"He knows us," Ares agrees, "but he *likes* her. Hannah should go with you, Andrus. I will stay in reserve. Lend me your cloak, and I can fly into attack position when I'm needed."

Hannah unfastens her purple cloak and reluctantly hands it to the God of War. "It's a gift from my father," she reminds him. "Take good care of it."

"I will." Ares fastens the cloak and adjusts the drape to keep his sword arm free. "If anything should happen, I will rain death from above."

"Thanks," I tell him. "I know I'll feel better knowing you've got our back. Just be careful with Mark's body, all right?"

Ares nods. "I am careful with all my vessels."

"I'm sure you are, but can you be extra-careful with Mark? He's not built for war like Mr. Cross."

Ares fixes me with his cold steel gaze. "I understand."

"So we've got the plan," Hannah says, "now we just need to make it happen."

I look down at the mossy cavern floor. "You mean *I* need to make it happen."

From across the field comes a bloodcurdling scream. The monsters are eating Mr. Cross, dividing him into torn and bloody pieces like some picnic of the damned.

There's no more time and nothing left to do. I sink to my knees and dig.

# 14

ANGER IS AN ENERGY

It's not enough to dig. I have to feel the earth, bond with it. Becoming one, and that oneness is what drives me forward. Down, through the dirt. Pushing, parting, plowing. The earth is my sister, the rocks are my brothers. They embrace me, they know me, then step aside. I angle the tunnel, creating as gentle slope as I can. It's working, and it's happening because I believe.

It's magic.

*I'm magic.*

The tunnel widens. It widens, and then we're through. Under the field, then under the Garden of Bone. We're almost there when I hit a wall of granite. A strange wall covered in mystic symbols. That stops me. I stare at the intricate glowing designs. Frustrated. Fascinated.

"This must be where they're hiding Cerberus," I say. "It's not like the rest of the rock around here. I can't seem to break through."

Hannah shines her flashlight on the wall and grimaces. "Damn it! Nothing's ever easy."

"I've broken magic wards before," I say. "The ones the priests left in Bronson Canyon."

"Those were to keep ghosts and monsters in the cave."

"So? Isn't this supposed to keep Cerberus in?"

"No, it's supposed to keep us out." Hannah runs her hand over the wall and quickly pulls it back as if stung. "No doubt there are similar wards on the inside for keeping Cerberus caged."

Above us, I hear the heavy taloned feet of Gyges stalking back and forth. The Lesser Titan shakes the tunnel with each step, driving home the danger we're in.

I lower my voice, even though I'm sure he can't hear us. "Can't you just break through with your magic?"

Hannah sighs. "How much do you know about magic, Andrus?"

"Not much. Everything I learned, I learned in the past few days."

"Then I'll keep this brief and basic: All magic is either sympathetic or antipathetic; it attracts or repels. But the most powerful magic, it combines these qualities to become something truly potent."

"You mean like this wall with one set of symbols on this side, and another set inside?"

"Exactly. These are symbols of antipathy, designed to keep us out. The other side will be covered in symbols of sympathy to keep Cerberus from wanting to leave. The best prison is one you don't want to escape from."

I think about that. I might think about it a lot more and a lot deeper, only this isn't the place and there's no time. "So what do we do? We can't just quit!"

"How are you feeling?" Hannah asks. "Your magic, I mean? You tired?"

"Not really. If anything, I feel stronger than when I started the tunnel."

"Interesting... Your power regenerates from contact with earth, and magic earth in particular. That's good."

"Because all the earth here is magic?"

"Not just that. This tunnel is made of magic earth, but it's earth you've used your magic on."

"So it's double magic?"

"In a sense, yes." She gives me an appraising look, then turns her attention back to the wall.

I get impatient watching her. I don't want to just stand here, I want to do something. "Maybe there are no symbols on the bottom. Maybe we can get in that way."

"No, Cronus will have thought of that. hang on, let me think."

I can feel my anger grow. I pace as much as the tunnel will let me to try and burn some of it off. It doesn't help. If anything, I seem to get more agitated. Finally, I can't take it anymore. "Look, let's just—"

"That's it!" Hannah says.

I stop and stare at her in confusion. "What?"

"Remember how your anger connected you to Cronus? And that let you read his thoughts?"

"Yeah."

"Well, you're angry now, right?"

"Sure, I'm angry! But I don't see what that has to do—"

"Magic wards like this are coded to keep things out or in, but they aren't coded to keep out whoever cast them."

"So? I'm not Cronus."

"No, you're not, but you're related to him, and if you knew anything about magic, you'd know that wards are weaker against those of the same bloodline as their caster."

"They sure seem to be strong enough against me."

Hannah smiles. ""Maybe you're not angry enough. Sure you don't want me to slap you? I don't mind. You have a very slappable face."

"Thanks, but no thanks. I can get plenty pissed off on my own."

Hannah bows and steps back, gesturing me to take her place at the wall. "Focus your anger, Andrus! Anger is an energy. Without focus, it's as dangerous to the wielder as to everyone around him. But if you can control it, you can use it, instead of it using you..."

I concentrate, first on my feelings, then on the wall. It cracks, and I feel its magic power wane. I pour pure molten hate into it, the hate of my father, and my hatred of him. The glowing symbols falter, flicker, and fade.

"Great job!" Hannah says from somewhere behind me, but it might as well be on the moon.

I can't stop the hate, can't stop the scream. I've tapped into something inside me. I've tapped into something *beyond* me. The cage wall shatters. I stand there, breathing hard, as six glowing red eyes swim out of the dark.

# 15

SOME THINGS ARE FOREVER

CERBERUS PADS FORWARD, eyes blazing, black fur bristling, but it's the fangs that really get my attention. There are so many of them! Of course there are. The monster dog has three heads, each equipped with an identical set of massive, snapping jaws.

I back up slowly. "N-nice dog," I stammer. "Good boy, Cerberus... Good boy!"

The hound of Hades barks and growls and snaps all at the same time.

"Hannah!" I half-shout, half-whisper. "I don't think he likes me. Do something! Now!" The big dog is ready to lunge, to take me in those foam-flecked teeth. On reflex, I unsheathe the crystal daggers from my knuckles.

Hannah steps forward, positioning herself between us. Cerberus lunges forward, bowling her over. She shrieks, and I raise my crystal spikes, but then I see the dog isn't biting her. He's licking her, slobbering with joy, and she's laughing and stroking his fur. I back off.

"It's OK!" Hannah says. "Cerberus is just happy to see me. Aren't you, boy?"

"If that's what he looks like when he's happy, I'd hate to see him mad."

Hannah gets up and takes a moment to scratch each of the black-furred heads behind the ears. "Who's a good dog? You want to help find Daddy?"

Cerberus nods his three heads vigorously and lets out several enthusiastic barks. Dust filters down from the ceiling, the tunnel walls vibrate as Gyges treads the ground above. All three of us eye the ceiling with mutual apprehension.

"We should go," Hannah says, hoisting herself up the monster dog's body. When she's seated behind the center head, she urges Cerberus forward. "Come on, boy!" Dog and rider leap forward, claws scrabbling against the tunnel floor.

I jog after them, but before I can break into a run, the tunnel ceiling collapses. A huge bird claw slams into my path. It's Gyges. I don't know if he knew we were down here or whether his weight accidentally collapsed the weakened ground above my tunnel. All I know is I'm cut off from Hannah and Cerberus. So I do the one thing, the only thing I can think of...

I jump onto the foot and jam my spikes into one of the orange toes, just above the talon. I'm not doing it to cause damage so much as to hold on when Gyges pulls his foot out of the hole. Which is exactly what the giant does, as its surprised bellow blasts my eardrums.

I'm lifted out of the tunnel in a shower of dirt and rock. Gyges yanks his monstrous leg up high and fast, taking me along for the ride. The world becomes a blur: the dizzying gem-starred ceiling above—a false sky under which harpies fly—and the Garden of Bone and centaurs and cyclopes below. All I know is I don't want to be on Gyges' foot when it lands.

*If I can time it just right...*

I jump off the second before the foot hits the ground, ducking into a roll that deposits me in front of Captain Nessus and the dismembered—but grotesquely still living—body of Mr. Cross. The centaur officer goggles at me with his gray-furred ram's face, not quite comprehending what he's seeing. I come out of my roll and immediately launch myself at Nessus. There's really no time to think of a better plan. And besides, I can see he has both of Ares' magic swords sheathed on his back.

I grab the swords free with a mighty *shing*, but before I can draw them across the centaur's throat, he bucks me off. I hit the ground hard, but not nearly as hard as I would have if I'd stayed glued to Gyges' foot.

Nessus brays orders in his inhuman goat-voice, rallying his centaur brothers Democ and Ruvo to his side, but that's not my only worry. The harpies circling above have caught on there's fresh meat. They take up a shrill chorus of "Give us the eyes! The eyes!" as they begin to peel off from their formation and launch into a dive. Claws thrust forward, greedy to taste the "juicy jewels" in my skull. There are more centaurs closing in.

I move in a defensive circle, blades out, seeking targets. I wish I hadn't lost my shield in my last battle with the Night Patrol, or I'd surely have it raised over my head to ward off the raking talons streaking down at me. But my blades and my reflexes are all I have, so I make use of them, slicing through a hideous harpy, sending the shrieking she-vulture away in a blast of blood and feathers. I'm almost immediately set on by another, but the centaurs are thrusting their hooked spears at me too, and it's all I can do to dodge both.

"Andrus Eaves!" Captain Nessus gives a gloating shout. "I have you now!"

"Not likely, you brain-eating bastard!" I lash out with my twin swords but the cruel beast gallops just out of reach.

His brothers, Democ and Ruvo, charge in, their flesh-hooking spears raised, and again, I'm forced to dodge rather than counterattack. The move puts me closer to a different centaur, one I don't know, and I waste no time chopping through his spear and into his hairy torso. Monster blood splashes my face: hot, black, and stinking. I wipe my forearm across my eyes to clear them, then I'm moving.

A cyclops lumbers toward me, swinging the jawbone of an animal like a club. The one-eyed giant is twenty feet tall, but I take him down by ducking under the clumsy swing and popping up inside his guard. The glowing blades sink into his groin, then slice through, pausing only briefly before severing the spine. The cyclops falls in two steaming pieces: guts spilling, gore gushing.

I'm breathing hard. I used up most of my magic busting Cerberus out of prison. I still have the three crystal daggers concealed in my right hand, but I'm saving those as a last resort.

I could really use Ares' help right about now because there is no clear path to escape, only different sets of monsters, with more coming in from all sides. I have to keep moving... cutting... cleaving. Where is Ares? Where are Hannah and Cerberus? Have they abandoned me?

I race through the Garden, using its hulking shards of bone as cover, until I run out of ways to go. I'm surrounded in a tight circle with nowhere to run.

"We have you now," Nessus gloats. "First, we eat the teacher, now the student!" His bold promise draws hungry howls and slobbering moans from the assembled creatures.

A cyclops smacks his club against his palm. "Smash him to paste!"

"No!" a harpy shrills. "Rip him to bits! To bits!"

There's a pillar of bone against my back, so I only have to worry about attack from three sides—and above.

But just as the monsters press forward, they fall back. The thunderous stomp of taloned feet tells me why: *Gyges wants a piece of me.* The fifty-headed giant looms like a nightmare, a thing that should not be, yet is. It forces the centaurs to widen their circle and scatters the flock of harpies, who resume their incessant circling—but far out of his reach.

Gyges doesn't attack. Instead, he seems to be laughing, though he has so many heads, it's hard to tell what some of them are doing. Can beasts laugh? They can certainly make noise. Some of the hundred arms rest at his sides, some clutch boulders or whale bones, while crab claws click and tentacles slither. But it is the central "face" in his torso that speaks, the one with the fanged and suckered mouth of a leech or lamprey, the one surrounded by the eight spider-like eyes.

"Little brother!" Gyges booms. "I am Gyges! Gyges the Reaver, Gyges the Invincible! The Destroyer! He of the Hundred Hands Who

Guards the Gate!" His voice is a storm, his words a horror. "You should not have come, not to me, nor to Tartarus. You must be very brave... or very foolish."

"Can't I be both?"

"You can," the giant agrees. "You can be many things all at once, like Gyges!" His other forty-nine heads growl, caw, bark, and hiss. "But you are something else, little brother! Something Gyges cannot be."

"What's that?"

"Desperate!" This gets a gruesome cheer from the monsters on his side. "Desperate, and alone!"

He's right about that, but instead I tell him, "We don't have to fight."

"No?" Gyges sneers scornfully. "What else is there but battle? Surrender, perhaps... Is that what you want, little brother? To surrender to Gyges? Because as much as I want to eat you, Cronus wants to eat you more, and Cronus is king."

"For now," I say. "Cronus is king for now, but not for always."

The many faces of Gyges take on a shrewd, appraising look—or whatever passes for it in their species. "Some things are forever," he says. "Some things are not. Who are you to say which is which?"

It's a fair question, and after a moment's hesitation, I answer. "I am Andrus Eaves, son of Cronus, son of Gaia, and I am a Titan!"

"You are," Gyges says, "but are you the Titan who will tear the crown from Cronus' head?"

"I am!"

"So!" Gyges says, his fifty faces erupting into toothy grins. "This you must prove! And you must do it without your friends, the Gods!" Some of his heads spit, others drool or drip venom. "You must do it by fighting me. There is no future without a fight!" The Lesser Titan thunders forward, monstrous mouths gaping, arms and weapons raised to crush, to rend, to destroy.

So much for diplomacy.

Panic grips me. I've never fought anything like Gyges before. The power, the sheer size of the thing overwhelms me. And knowing I'm related to it makes it worse.

I bring my swords up in what feels like a futile gesture, ready for the end. The inevitable. If I can't hope to defeat Gyges, how can I hope to defeat Cronus?

As I stare up in horror, I see a familiar fog billow from the ceiling. A fog that takes on the form of Ares, God of War. He materializes in front of the onrushing giant, sword out. Gyges runs right into it, but of course, it's just a pin prick to a creature that size. No, it's what Ares does that gets Gyges to notice.

He tugs the blade down, peeling through the giant's flesh like a blood-red zipper, cutting the chest open from the breast bone to the ribs. When he gets to the central face in the torso where the thing's stomach should be, he kicks in one of the spider eyes to add insult to injury. Gyges screams, fifty screams from fifty throats in one fearsome sound. Yellow fluid slimes thickly from the cratered eye.

Ares uses his feet to push off from the injured giant, executing a perfect gymnastics move. The God of War lands on the moss-green cavern floor next to me. "My swords!" he says. It's not a question, it's a command. I hand the blades to him, and he hands me his.

"You should clean that," he says.

"What?" That's when I notice the yellow slime clinging to the blade is eating through the metal. Before I can think how to wipe it off, the blade doesn't just sizzle, it melts.

"Scratch that," Ares says. "You'll need a new sword." He hands me one of his. "Here, this one won't melt."

Gyges staggers sideways, all pretense at a charge done. Instead, it's become an agonized stumble, then a drunken fall as he trips over the bones blocking his path and narrowly avoids impaling himself on one. Titans really can be hurt. And if they can be hurt, they can be killed. That is, once we free Hades and bring Death back into the world...

Captain Nessus attempts to rally the demoralized horde of monsters. Gyges is rolling around on the ground, a tangle of thrashing limbs and kicking claws, and part of me dares to hope he won't be getting up again. But to my horror, the long red wound in his chest is knitting shut. Slowly, probably painfully, but still, Gyges is healing.

I let out a long breath. "I didn't know he could do that…"

"You don't know a lot of things," Ares says. "Let's make sure you live to find them out." He unfastens Hannah's magic cloak and hands it to me. "You should go now. Hannah needs your help."

"What about you?" I ask as Captain Nessus leads his monsters toward us.

"I'm the God of War," Ares says. "Good odds, bad odds. Doesn't matter. I live for this."

"I know you do," I say, "and thanks for the save, but remember your promise to take care of Mark."

Ares nods. "I'll do what I can. Go to the boulder; Shadow will be waiting for you. He'll lead you to Hannah. And be careful when you decide to change out of fog form; the cloak only works three times a day and this is the last time."

My last view of Ares may be my last view of Mark. "Thanks," I say, "to both of you… for everything."

The monsters close in, and as they do, I will myself to turn to fog. I float away to the clash of steel and cries of war.

# 16

INTUITION

BEING IMMATERIAL IS BEYOND WEIRD. It's terrifying, yet also liberating, and I wonder if this is how ghosts feel. This seems a lot closer to what it must be like to be dead than being in Charon's boat. Like anything, I suppose you get used to it after a while, but I don't think I ever could. Not to this. I'd miss feeling connected to the Earth.

Behind me, the battle rages, but it's hard to focus on that. Every time I do, I stop moving, and if there's one thing I need, it's to move as fast and far as I can.

*Please, let Mark be OK...*

*Please, let this not have all been for nothing.*

After seeing what Ares did, I wish I could have fought Gyges. I feel like I have something to prove... not to the giant, but to myself. That I am that powerful. That I can do this—and whatever comes after.

When I get to the edge of the mushroom forest, Shadow is waiting. Hannah's raven is perched in a tree overlooking the boulder and the tunnel I made. Enormous paw prints dot the mossy cavern floor. That's going to be a problem. I know I shouldn't transform back to flesh yet, but it won't take long for the monsters to track Cerberus if I don't do something about these prints.

Shadow cocks his black feathered head as I turn solid as if to say, "What are you doing?"

"I'm going to erase the tracks," I tell the bird, hoping he'll telepathically let Hannah know. Then, under my breath, I add, "If I can." I've never tried to do anything like this before, and I know I don't have much magic left, but just having my feet back on the ground is helping.

I give it a minute, then kneel down and press my palms to the earth. It turns out erasing tracks is a lot easier than digging tunnels or breaking through enchanted stone walls. The depressions lift up, the earth restoring itself to its original, unblemished condition. Maybe learning to master my magic is as simple as intuition—knowing what makes sense for me and what doesn't.

"Did you see that?" I ask the raven.

It bobs its head enthusiastically, then flies down from its perch to the next set of prints, pointing with its beak. I erase those tracks, and the next, but this seems like an inefficient way to do it.

"You think I could erase a bunch of tracks all at once?" I ask the bird.

It caws and opens its wings, as if to say it's not sure, but it's a good idea to try it. I concentrate, going deeper into the earth this time, going farther, reaching out... I shut my eyes and see the tracks in my mind. I will them to vanish.

*Restore the earth... Restore, and let no tracks remain...*

When I open my eyes, the tracks are gone. Of course, I can't see how far ahead my magic has worked, but I'm happy with the result. Happy enough to try one more experiment...

I rub dirt on the bottoms of my boots, and I imagine that it's magic dirt, limitless dirt that hides my tracks, filling in my footprints as I travel. Then I get up and test it. It works!

I cast a final look at the Garden of Bone. One last look at the battle I can't tell who's winning. I'd pray for Mark, but I don't know who to pray to now that Cronus is my enemy and Zeus is dead. Mark had said maybe after all this, he'd become a priest of me, but it doesn't feel right praying to myself.

What God or Titan does that?

That leaves Gaia, the Earth Mother. *My mother.* So I say a prayer to her. I thank her for my life, and my power. I thank her for protecting me and my friends.

There is no divine revelation, no nurturing voice from on high or down deep, but I do feel better afterward, even more connected—not just to the Earth, but to myself. *To what I am.* The more I admit it, the more I accept it, the more powerful I become.

Shadow flies up and flaps overhead.

"OK, buddy," I tell the familiar. "We're done here. Take me to Hannah."

# 17

## THE LEDGE

FAR BEHIND, I hear the cruel cry of harpies, the hoofbeats of centaurs. The sounds of my enemies ring in my ears, driving me on. Between the tree-sized mushrooms granting me cover and my magic erasing Cerberus' tracks, I don't think I'm being followed. Not yet, anyway.

I'm glad Ares didn't abandon me, though I understand why Hannah did. After everything we'd done to break Cerberus free, for her to charge back into the Garden would have been stupid. I can't find Hades without the three-headed dog, and without her and Shadow, I'd be lost in Tartarus forever—or until Cronus and his minions caught me.

The forest thins. There's less and less cover. The ground gets rougher, the angle steeper, but the change in terrain means it should be hard, if not impossible, for the centaurs to follow. Then again, they're part goat, so maybe that's not as true as I'd like it to be.

All I know is I better find some cover soon, or regardless of the centaurs, the harpies will be sure to spot me. I climb a hill to a high enough vantage point where I can see over the the top of the mushroom forest, but I can't make out the Garden of Bone. What I should be able to see is Gyges towering over everything, but I don't see the bastard anywhere. That's a relief, and it isn't.

I haven't known the giant long, but from our brief interaction, I know he's a lot smarter than I initially gave him credit for. It's hard to imagine anything that ugly could be intelligent, but after my dealings with Nessus, I know how cunning monsters can be. I'm guessing Gyges is either busy chasing Ares or has gone off to reinforce wherever they're hiding Hades.

For one brief, crazy moment, I consider doubling back to see if I can pick up Gyges' tracks and follow him, but Hannah's waiting. Besides, there are too many monsters combing the area, and if Gyges is anything like me, he's probably erasing his footprints as well. So there's no way to go except forward.

*The one way, the only way. Toward fate, toward destiny...* As always, it's the long way, the hard way, with not much room for error.

The dog's paw prints are gone now thanks to the hillside's rocky terrain. I check the sky for Shadow, but the raven is nowhere in sight. The going gets tougher, but I'm at my best climbing rock, so I take a few vertical shortcuts. These take me straight up a sheer cliff, and for a moment, I can pretend I'm not in Tartarus. I'm back home, off for a weekend adventure without a worry in the world... It's a nice fantasy, while it lasts.

Above me is a ledge draped in corpse-white moss. I heave myself up and find myself face to face with Cerberus. The three-headed beast growls, but one sharp "Heel!" from Hannah shuts him down. The dog backs up, giving me room to clamber over the side. There's a cave at the back of the ledge.

I lay on my back panting while Hannah and Cerberus stand over me. One of the black-furred heads gives my face an experimental lick, then makes a disgusted face. I laugh and push the head away, then sit up. "Where's your bird?"

"Sent him to keep watch around the perimeter."

"Oh. I had to guess where you were."

"So? You guessed right."

I don't have anything to say to that. The witch infuriates me sometimes, but there's something I like about her.

"Where's Ares?" Hannah asks.

"Don't know. Told me to run. Guess he wanted all the glory for himself."

"More like he wanted to save your ass. I'll take my cloak back now, if you don't mind."

I hand it over and she fastens it around her shoulders. "Thanks, I felt naked without it."

"Not big on sharing, are you?"

"Not really. I was an only child."

"Come on! I find that hard to believe."

Hannah snorts. "I am now. Hades had other children, of course. You can't be alive as long as him without fathering a few. They're all dead. It was the war... The damned war."

"So you're the last?"

She nods, staring out at the gloomy horizon. "Ares, son of Zeus, and Hannah, daughter of Hades. We're the last of our kind, the legacy of Mount Olympus and all it stood for..."

"You think Ares made it?"

"He's tough."

"Tough enough to beat Gyges?"

Hannah shrugs and turns away. "We should get some rest and stay out of sight. Shadow will keep watch."

I follow her and Cerberus into the cave. She hands me an energy bar and water bottle from her pouch. We eat in silence.

"You think Mark's going to be all right?"

"Andrus," Hannah says, "worrying about your friend, worrying about anyone or anything beyond the quest won't help. Believe me, I know."

"So you're not worried about Ares?"

"I'm worried about *the quest*. If it fails, then all the things we care about won't matter. So go ahead and care, but don't worry. Worry only gets in the way. Now get some sleep; we've got a long day ahead." She turns away and snuggles into Cerberus, using the monster dog as both pillow and blanket.

I sit there a while, watching her while Cerberus watches me. Eventually, the dog closes its big red eyes and I close mine.

## 18

---

THE LABYRINTH OF DREAMS

WHEN I OPEN MY EYES, I'm not in the cave. Not with Hannah, or Cerberus, or Shadow. I'm alone in a vast underground labyrinth. Stone walls fence me in, angling down, funneling me toward the center. But the center of what? The maze? The Earth? Tartarus, or somewhere beyond?

The walls are wet and mossy, dripping with slime, and it's cold here, the cold of the grave, but it's getting warmer with every step. I hit a few dead ends and have to turn around. I think I hear a voice, no more than a whisper, calling my name.

*"Andrus... Come closer!"*

The voice is both familiar and unfamiliar. One part welcoming, one part mocking. Daring me to find its owner. Daring me down, into the depths...

*"Andrus..."*

I hit another dead end, and this time, the voice laughs. There's a skeleton embedded in the wall, half-buried, and more than that, half-melted into the stone. No, not melted. *Digested.*

I back away, followed by the laughter. The next path I pick takes a steep downward grade, and the stone floor beneath me becomes a ramp too slick to stand on. I start to slide, then fall. Desperately, I reach out, extending the crystal daggers from my knuckles. Punching them into the floor. I stop falling and hang there.

"Who are you?" I yell. "What do you want?"

The laughter gets louder. The floor cracks and crumbles. I'm falling again, falling into darkness with nothing to catch or break my fall. It reminds me of the many dreams I've had—dreams of climbing Mount Olympus, only now it's in reverse. I'm falling from a great height, falling into Tartarus, falling into punishment. And maybe it's one I deserve for failing to protect my parents, and Lucy, and Mark...

A spot of red and orange light appears below. The air grows hot. I'm falling into the labyrinth's molten core. There's no escape, nothing I can do. I splash down into fire, blasted by heat, baked by lava. I struggle to swim up and when I break the surface, I see I'm not in the center of the Earth or Tartarus or anywhere else. I'm in the center of an enormous stomach and the "lava" is acid. Agonized half-living corpses thrash and scream in the vile orange soup.

*I'm inside Cronus.*

*I'm inside the place that gave me my power.*

When I look down at my hands, I see rock. When I look at my arms, I see rock. Every part of me is rock. And I'm not being digested, like the other victims bubbling beside me. I'm absorbing power. This is both my prison and my womb, the long slow process of my birth, forged from nothing, fed on hate.

*Hate and magic.*

I feel the rage of Cronus, I feel his hunger.

And then I'm being vomited up. I don't want to go, yet I must. I didn't have a choice asking to be made, just like I don't have a choice asking to be born.

I land in a puddle of sickly goo on a hot stone floor. My body is no longer made of rock, at least not the kind you can see. I look human. I feel human, or however I think being human feels. I'm in a cave, beside a lake of fire.

Cronus is watching. Cronus is here!

The King of the Titans towers over me, wearing a crown of horns. His skin is red, covered in black-tinged scales, each as large as a warrior's shield. His mouth is wide, his teeth fanged. The eyes are the worst. There are three of them, each one a blazing ring, with the intensity of looking into the sun. Cronus reminds me of a dragon, of man and dragon merged into one, grown to nightmare size. He has no wings though, no tail, no forked tongue. His powerful arms and feet end in claws. He lunges forward, a living volcano screaming hate and fire.

I take the blast and stand before him, undamaged. Adrenalized, but not unafraid. "Hello, father," I say as bravely as I can.

Cronus's black lips twist into what can only be described as a smile—the most hideous one I've ever seen. "Andrus, my son! Home, at last."

"I'm here to stop you."

Cronus laughs, the same laughter I heard before. "You can try. All my children try, and all my children fail, because they are only a shadow of my power."

"I'm more than a shadow!"

The blazing trio of eyes narrow. "So you are, son! That is why I talk to you. That is why you must listen..."

"Listen? Listen to what?"

"To my offer. You have come far, but you are still young, still foolish, still too much a man, when you could be so much more."

"You mean a Titan?"

"Yes! Accept your place among us. Do not put your trust in the Gods. They will use you, betray you, as they have ever done to our kind."

"So I should trust you instead? But you want to kill me!"

Cronus smirks. "I want to kill the weakness in you. I want to test you, to see the true you, the glorious you! I want to see the Titan in you, and the son who can stand at my side."

"Why? Why not kill me like Zeus and all the rest?"

"Because you are different, Andrus. *Special.* Your mother, Gaia, is my mother too. She wanted you to be born. To make peace. Peace between the Titans and the Gods. And there can be..."

"How?"

"How else can we have peace? The Gods must die! Kill them, Andrus. Kill the Gods and let the war be done. Prove your worth! Prove you are truly my son, my prince, my heir. Prove you are a Titan and all this can be yours!"

Cronus' eyes flare into blinding arcs, and I see portals in them, portals to other places, other worlds. Worlds untouched by Gods or men. Beautiful worlds, terrible worlds, and worlds beyond imagining. A universe full of possibilities.

"But how? Why do you need me?"

"Because you are the bridge, Andrus. The Bridge Between Worlds! It is true you were formed from rock, but not a rock of Earth, or even Tartarus. You were a rock that fell from the sky—a meteor. A union of Earth and Sky, forged in my heat. That makes you my son, my brother, and my hope!"

"Hope for what?"

"For new worlds to conquer! You can open that door, Andrus. You can open it and travel through as my emissary. Take whatever mortals you want with you: your foster parents, Mark, Lucy. I will give them to you, and I can give you so much more!"

"But only if I side with you?"

"You are a Titan," Cronus says. "Blood calls to blood, family to family, father to son. I am not your enemy unless you make me one."

"But you're evil..."

"Evil? What do you know of evil? You have not suffered as I have, have not known the pain of a thousand betrayals! You do not wear the scars of a thousand battles, nor the despair of eternity. It's true, I turned on my other children, the same way my father turned on me. But they wanted my world because they could not have another! You... You aren't like them. You can have your own world, dozens of them!"

"As long as I rule in your name?"

Cronus nods. "Yes, for only I can show you what must be done! Only I can teach you. *And I will teach you, Andrus.* How hard the lessons are is up to you."

"What about Hades? You don't want me to free him?"

"On the contrary, I want you to do what you think is best, and see the result."

"But I thought you wanted Hades imprisoned? Without Death, the human sacrifices would last forever..."

"There are reasons beyond reasons. After the destruction of most of the Earth in the Gods War, the scheme to suspend the power of Death was necessary in order to ration the remaining human population."

"And now?"

"Humanity is rebuilding, but I grow weary of the same food. I hunger for new tastes in new worlds! You can give me that, Andrus. You *will* give me that!"

"Or else what?"

"Or else what, indeed!" The greedy lips peel back, revealing row after row of fangs, like the mouth of a shark. "Do not test my patience. Go now, go forth on your quest, but know that you do so at my pleasure, and my command! Once you see what Hades is really like... once you see how badly you have been used by the Gods, then you will come to Cronus. You shall come freely, and I will be here, where I always am: *Inside you. Waiting. Watching.* Now go!"

With a wave of his hand, I'm gone.

# PART II

TO FREE A GOD

# 19

BORN TO POWER

I WAKE, heart hammering. Hannah is asleep, but at least one of Cerberus' heads isn't. The muzzle raises, the red eyes slowly open.

"Good boy," I whisper.

Cerberus stares at me, then yawns. I get a good look inside his fanged mouth before he's done. The head lowers, the eyes close. I walk out of the cave onto the hillside, the dream still fresh in my mind. I look out over the weird forest below, arms crossed against the chill sense of dread crawling up my spine. I have no doubt some of what Cronus said was lies, but some of it felt true.

*The offer felt true.*

Cronus wants me to free Hades so he can kill him... and Hannah, and Ares. With no Gods left to fight or imprison, the war would be over then. The Titans would be free. Free to rule, free to reign forever.

I can save my foster parents. I can save Mark and Lucy... *And I can have power!* Power in a new world where I decide what's right and wrong. Where I control who lives and dies. Except I wouldn't, not really. Cronus would, and he's got a pretty poor track record valuing life—human or otherwise. But maybe I can find a way to make it work, to shut him out. But how can I keep the King of the Titans out of my world when I can't even keep him out of my dreams?

I'm so lost in my thoughts, I don't even hear Hannah creep up on me until she's at my side. "Couldn't sleep?"

I shake my head. "Bad dream."

"You get those a lot?"

"Sometimes. More lately."

"What was it about?" Hannah asks, her eyes intense.

"Cronus."

She nods. "The barriers are less restrictive here."

"The barriers to what?"

"To telepathy, astral projection. Dream manipulation."

I don't say anything.

Hannah shrugs. "He made you an offer, didn't he?"

"Yes."

"Look, Andrus, you said 'no more secrets,' remember?"

"Yeah, I remember. Only I guess it's not so easy when they're mine."

She smiles, not unkindly. "Now you know how I feel. Our fathers are... complicated. They expect us to keep their secrets, yet keep none of our own."

"Yeah, it sucks. In the dream, Cronus told me some things... things about myself."

"Do you want to tell me?"

"I don't know. Can I trust you?"

Her dark eyes find mine. "Can I trust you?"

I heave a sigh out over the ledge and in that moment, I make my decision. "Cronus says he wants us to free Hades so he can kill him."

She laughs, and that's not the reaction I expect.

"What's so funny? I just told you he wants us to free your dad so he can murder him! So he can murder Ares and you."

"I know, but what choice do we have? Freeing my father is my only hope to stop Cronus. My only chance for any kind of..."

"Normal life?"

"My life is never going to be normal, Andrus. Neither is yours. It can't. Like it or not, we were born to power. We were born to change the world."

*Or bridge it*, I think to myself, then shove the thought aside. It's one thing to find out I'm a magic rock, and another to find out I'm an alien one, a meteor. The Bridge Between Worlds... I haven't even had time to process the first revelation before Cronus hit me with another and another.

*Why?* Why tell me now, or at all? To keep me reeling. Off-balance. And maybe to tip me over from Hannah's side to his...

"Gods and Titans," I say. "Titans and Gods! Where does it end? When one side murders the other? Is that the only way we can have peace?"

Hannah rests her hand on my shoulder. "No side is all good, Andrus, or all evil. Some of the Gods were just as bad as the Titans, and some of the Titans were as good as the best of the Gods."

"And me?" I ask.

She grins. "The jury's still out."

"Is it?" I'm painfully aware how close she is, how beautiful.

"Yeah." The word is a whisper, the silence that follows a promise.

I am the Bridge Between Worlds. What if that doesn't just mean to other worlds, but to other possibilities within our own? What if I am the bridge between Gods and Titans? What if that's the reason Gaia plucked me from the stars and brought me to life? What if that's the reason I'm here? *What if, what if...* My thoughts crumble, my reason flees, and for good reason.

Hannah's lips are on mine. It's like a spell—a spell where I can't think, only feel. There's an energy between us, a connection that goes beyond the physical. Beyond boy and girl. The heat rises in me, the air between us steaming with more than our breath. It's magic. *We're magic.* And that scares me, but not enough to stop.

## 20

---

### A BATTLE I CAN'T WIN

I break away from the kiss. For something that felt so good, it hurts. It hurts to end it, and I'm tempted to go back for more. To stop the pain as much as to feel the pleasure, to renew the connection. Instead, I step back and say, "We can't." It doesn't sound very convincing, not to her and not to me.

"Do you mean can't or shouldn't?" Hannah closes the gap between us.

I shake my head. "I don't know. Both?"

"Because of Lucy?"

"Because of a lot of things. Us being together would only complicate things."

Hannah nods. "OK."

"You sure?"

"I was only kissing you out of pity anyway," she teases.

"You sure about that?" I ask. "It felt pretty mutual to me."

"How many girls have you kissed, Andrus?"

"I don't know," I lie. "A lot."

"Uh-huh. You've kissed exactly one in the time I've been watching you. Two now, counting me."

"I've never been good with people. I'm not sure I can be."

"Because you're a Titan?"

I shrug.

"You wanna know a secret? I've never been very good with people either."

"Because you're a Demigoddess?"

She laughs. "No, Andrus, because I'm a bitch."

"I was going to say, 'witch.'"

"Yeah, well, that too. Magic never left me much time for anything else, or anyone..."

"I was like that with sports, but I preferred the kind I could do alone."

"Rock climbing," Hannah says. "Spelunking. That makes sense, considering what you are."

"What I am..." I echo, letting the words wander through my mind. "I didn't ask for any of this."

"No one does, Andrus, but we get it anyway. Some of us more than others."

"Like you?"

"Like us." She kisses me again, pressing her slim body against mine. This time, I don't push her away. This time, I let it happen. "After we free my father," she whispers in my ear, "anything can happen... We could die, and I don't want to die—not with regrets." Her mouth works on mine, petal-soft, yet with the fierceness of a thousand lonely nights, a thousand lonely dreams.

I match her passion. Hannah is a battle I can't win, so I don't even try.

# 21

GODS DON'T APOLOGIZE

WE'RE INTERRUPTED by a crash of wings. At first, I think the harpies have found us, but it's only Shadow. The raven flies between us, forcing me back. It lands on Hannah's outstretched arm, cawing loudly.

"What is he, jealous?" I ask.

"No, it's Ares," she says. "Shadow found him. He's on his way up."

An insistent scrabbling comes from below as we compose ourselves. A moment later, the God of War appears at the ledge. I offer him a hand as he climbs over the side. "This vessel wasn't made for such exertion," Ares complains. When Hannah and I don't answer, but look at each other longingly, he barks short laughter. "Not interrupting anything, am I?"

Hannah blushes, and I feel the color rush to my cheeks.

"What happened?" I say to change the subject. "You all right?"

Mark's body is bloody and battered, covered in nasty scrapes and bruises. His clothes are torn, his hair hangs in greasy clumps. Ares pops his joints, then cracks his neck from side to side. When he's satisfied, he says, "The vessel is intact. The cyclopes are dead."

"What about Gyges?" I ask.

"I led the bastard on a merry chase, but with this vessel's limitations, I regret I could not do more."

That's about what I expected, and probably the best outcome we could have hoped for, all things considered. The important thing is Ares is OK, and so is Mark. "I wish you'd stop calling Mark your 'vessel.' He's my friend."

"Understood," the War God says. "And you're right. Mark has served us well, and continues to serve. We trained his body well, you and I. If only we'd had more time, if only he hadn't been so resistant in class..."

"Mark was the kind of guy who always lived more in his head than his body." I cringe, realizing I just referred to Mark in the past tense. "Anyway, Mark really isn't so different from me. He was just more into thinking, while I was more into doing."

"There is a time for thought and a time for action," Ares muses. "Both have their place in war. Not every man must be in the frontlines to attain glory; generals, engineers, and medics have their place as well."

"And priests," I add.

Ares grunts. "If you say so. I've always found them to be a necessary evil."

"That's a funny thing to say coming from a God."

"Not really," Hannah says. "Priests presume too much... They expect divine intervention in life, a place of honor at their deity's side in death. My father had no use for priests. That's why I'm a witch. I don't depend on anyone to answer my prayers but me."

"Not that there's anyone left to answer," Ares says. "Your father was wise to train you in the use of magic."

Hannah nods. "He knew what was coming, but no one would listen, not until it was too late..."

"And then the war," Ares says grimly.

"And then the war," she agrees.

"At least we're still here," I say to lighten the mood. "At least we're still fighting. More glory for us, right?"

"Well said, Andrus." Ares draws his sword, raising it over our heads. "To us! To the fighters, and to victory! May it be swift and glorious."

"*To victory!*" Hannah and I echo, and we raise our blades to his, holding them there. Savoring the moment. Drawing strength from it.

It's a welcome thrill, good for morale, but it doesn't last long. I wish I knew what to do about Cronus, about Hannah and Lucy and everything. But I don't, so I fill Ares in on what I told Hannah about my dream.

"I'm not surprised," Ares says when I'm done. "I appreciate you telling me."

"There's something else," I say.

Hannah frowns. "Something you didn't mention before?"

I sigh. "I wanted to, only it's all so new, I was still processing it, and then... I, uh, had other things on my mind."

"We both did," Hannah agrees. "So what weren't you telling me?"

Hearing the three of us, Cerberus pokes its heads out of the cave, then pads over to Ares and gives him a few experimental sniffs. Ares reaches out and ruffles the dog's fur. It's tongues loll in pleasure.

"Andrus?" Hannah prods. "You were saying?"

"Have you ever heard of something called the Bridge Between Worlds?"

Ares stops petting the dog. Hannah looks at me, her raven adjusting its perch on her forearm. "We've heard of it," she says.

I shift uncomfortably. "What is it?"

"It's the end of the Titans," Ares say. "A weapon. The Bridge is a way to bring peace and security to the remaining Gods, and by killing the Titans, the Bridge will have the power to open new worlds for us."

"Cronus said it was a way to do that, but for the Titans. For him, in particular, and that it would kill the Gods."

Ares and Hannah exchange a look. "It's an old prophecy, Andrus, and subject to interpretation."

"So you both could be right? About the Bridge being able to kill one side to secure peace and prosperity for the other?"

Ares scowls, his eyes flashing gold. "Gods are never wrong, Andrus."

Hannah steps between us. "Except when they are. Even you have made a few errors in your time, and don't get me started on Zeus and Hera!"

Ares scoffs and folds his arms across his chest, but makes no move to contradict her. The gesture would have been more impressive had the God still been possessing Mr. Cross. In Mark's body, it looks slightly ridiculous, but I know better than to doubt the War God's power.

"Andrus," Hannah says, "what exactly did Cronus tell you about the Bridge Between Worlds? Does he have it? Does he know where to find it? The Gods and Titans have been looking for the Bridge for thousands of years, but no one's ever found it."

Neither of them know I am the Bridge. They think the Bridge is a place, or a thing, not a person. Not me. But I was born from rock, and a rock is a thing. And I come from a place—a place beyond the stars, one nobody could find until the time was right. So I tell them, "Cronus doesn't have the Bridge. He knows where it is, though. He wants me to get it."

"Why can't he get it himself?" Ares asks.

"Because he needs me to do it."

"You?" Hannah asks. "Why you?"

"I'm not sure... I guess because nobody else can access it."

Cerberus whines, and Ares absently pats the monster on its nearest head. "Andrus, if this is true, then the power to end this war rests with you."

"I thought it lay with Hades?"

"Hades is part of it," Hannah says. "Without him being free to loose Death on the world, maybe the Bridge can't be accessed, or can't be used. What do you think, cousin?"

Ares frowns. "I think the Bridge must be bathed in the blood of the enemy. I'm not speaking poetically, either. I mean literally drenched in the juices of the dying."

Hannah's dark eyes light up. "Releasing all that magic at once must open the Bridge."

"And then we go through," Ares says. "We go through and reap the bounty of new worlds, young worlds unspoiled in their beauty. The home of a new Olympus!"

"An Olympus without the mistakes of the past," Hannah adds.

"Wait a minute, you guys! What about Earth? I thought we were doing this for humanity?"

"We are," Hannah says, "but we're also doing it for ourselves. There are millions of humans left, but only three Olympians: Hades, Ares, and myself."

"Half-Olympian," Ares corrects her. "You had a human mother."

Hannah's face darkens with anger. "Really, cousin? You think now is a good time to bring up my parentage? As if I haven't done at least as much as you to make our victory happen? Maybe more! And you, you're only an avatar—a shadow of your former glory!"

"It seems I struck a nerve," Ares says. "Let us move on before the situation becomes disagreeable."

"You should apologize," I tell him.

Ares smirks. "Gods don't apologize, Andrus. And even if they did, War never does."

Hannah rolls her eyes. "You can see why nobody likes him."

"Oh? As if they liked your father any better?"

"*Anyway,*" Hannah says, loud enough to make her point, "Andrus, do you know where the Bridge is?"

I don't like the ugly way the conversation has turned, so I decide not to tell them I'm the Bridge. At least not yet. I don't know if it's paranoia or common sense. Maybe both.

"Andrus?" Hannah asks again. "Well, do you know?"

"No, but if the Bridge is a weapon that can destroy the remaining Gods or Titans, what if it could be used to kill just *some* of them?"

Ares' brow knits in confusion. "Some? Why would we only kill some? Half a victory is no victory at all. It is a defeat!"

"I'm just saying... what if they're not all bad?"

Ares runs a bloody hand through his matted hair. "Not all bad? How would you know? How many Titans have you met besides Gyges and Cronus?"

Hannah says, "I think he means Prometheus..."

Ares groans. "What, him? Bah! That trickster had his uses, but he was nothing but trouble! Zeus was right to punish him."

"What about me?" I ask. "I have my uses, but what about after we free Hades?"

Ares says, "You'll help us secure the Bridge, and use it to wipe out the Titans."

"What if that wipes me out too?" I ask.

The two Olympians exchange a look. Hannah says, "Then we wouldn't use it."

Ares doesn't seem so convinced. "War is sacrifice! I sacrificed the greater portion of my power, and the others... my father, my mother, my brothers and sisters... they gave everything."

"So you'd be willing to sacrifice me?" I ask.

"Andrus..." Hannah lays a hand on my arm, but I shrug it off.

"No!" I say. "No, let him answer."

Ares says, "If there was a way to preserve you, we would."

"And if there wasn't?"

The War God shrugs. "You would have a decision to make: to sacrifice yourself or not."

"And that's just it, isn't it? It would be *my decision!* And what if I chose to do what I wanted?"

Hannah says, "I know this is a confusing time for you, but the Titans are your enemy as much as ours. Haven't we been good to you? Haven't we trained you, fought at your side?"

"Yes, and I'm grateful. Don't think that I'm not! But if this Bridge is some ultimate weapon, I want to use it right."

"You will," Hannah says. "I know you will." She gives me an encouraging smile.

"We should rest," Ares says. "Tomorrow, we free Hades." He stalks into the cave, followed by Cerberus.

Hannah watches until the cave swallows them, then turns to me. "Ares likes to finish what he starts," she says as if to apologize. "I don't know if you noticed, but he can be kind of a dick, and damn, is he stubborn."

"You're telling me! I thought he was this great guy before."

"He still is, in his own way. It's not always a nice way, or an easy way, but in a fight, there's no one else you want by your side."

"What about the rest of the time?" I ask.

"He has his moments. But there's reasons he's the way he is, and not just the usual ones. There's more to it than that..."

"Yeah? Like what?"

"He lost so much in the war, and more than that, he lost his pride. How great a God of War can you be when your side loses? He had one job, Andrus, and that was to win."

"I guess I hadn't thought of it that way."

"The only thing that keeps Ares going is we have one last chance, one last shot for his redemption... redemption and revenge. Ares can be hard and cruel, but he's exactly what we need. That's why I let him get away with his little temper tantrums. That's why you should too."

"The fragile male ego?" I joke.

Hannah snorts. "Something like that, but times a million. He is a God, after all."

"Correction, he's an avatar."

She grins. "Taking my side already? I must have trained you well."

"Ha, ha. I'm just worried... I don't know where I fit after this is all over."

Hannah puts her arm around me. "You belong with us."

"Us?"

"Fine, *with me*, for however long you can stand it." We kiss, then sit on the ledge, dangling our feet over the side. "I get it, you know."

"What?"

"Why you want to save Prometheus," she says. "I think you want to save him because you think he's different, like you. And because you want a family."

"I have a family. My human parents, remember?"

"An extended family, then. A magical one, so you wouldn't feel so alone. I know all about human parents. I had a human mother, so I know what that's like, and how they can never fully understand what it's like to be a God."

"Demigod."

"Demigoddess," Hannah corrects me, then leans in for a kiss. "But I'm no Aphrodite."

"No, you're not."

She gives me a playful punch. "I can't believe you said that. You're such a jerk!"

I chuckle. "I meant you're better than her."

"Why's that?" Her face drifts close.

"Because the Goddess of Love wouldn't make out with me."

"You're pretty smart for a rock."

"I'm pretty sexy too."

"Yeah," she whispers. "Yeah, Rock Boy, you are…"

## 22

WE'RE ALL MURDERERS

THE NEXT MORNING, we set off from the hillside. The forest, already thin in this part, gives way to a harsh, broken land. Cerberus leads the way, snuffling the barren ground for the scent of his lost master.

The dog-beast seems confused at first, sending us in circles until I begin to wonder if he can find the path at all. Ares also becomes impatient, though our mutual anger does little to bond us after last night's argument. Only Hannah remains confident, and it is her confidence that pays off.

"He's found it!" Hannah exclaims as Cerberus bounds ahead. "He's picked up the scent!"

As we hurry to catch up, I ask, "How can you be sure? What if he just smelled some prey or something?"

"This whole kingdom smells of my father. It took Cerberus some time to separate the general scent from the specific. Hey, I've been meaning to ask you..." Hannah pants as we race along.

"What?" I puff back.

"If Cronus wants us to free my father, then why's he making it so hard?"

"Good question," Ares agrees.

"He's testing me," I reply. "I guess to make me reveal my powers...

I think this is all a game to him, and besides, if he made the quest too easy, we'd suspect something was wrong."

"Makes sense," Hannah says. "Boy, look at Cerberus go!"

The three-headed beast is bounding along a river bed. It's only as we get closer to it that I notice the river is red. "Call him back!"

"What?" Hannah gasps "Why?"

"That river! It's full of blood!"

"It's nothing."

"Nothing? You call that nothing?"

"It's just the run-off from Murder Town."

I don't know what to say to that. I don't know what there is to say, what any sane mind could think of. But this isn't Earth, this is Tartarus, the Kingdom of the Dead, so why shouldn't there be a river of blood? Maybe that's the most normal thing here.

"It's called Acheron," Hannah explains. "The River of Woe. Remember, I told you it's what separates the good half of Tartarus from the bad?"

"I don't think we should go near it."

Hannah laughs. "Chicken!"

"Next, you'll be telling me some of your best friends are murderers." I steal a quick glance at Ares, not wanting to give offense, but then realize we're all murderers.

"We all kill," Hannah says. "You, me, Ares... Every God and Titan kills. It's the reason why you kill that matters."

We're jogging along now, just trying to keep Cerberus in sight.

"Morality," Ares says, breaking his silence, "is different for us, Andrus. It's less fixed, more situational. There is duty—your moral duty to defend your kind against enemies—then there is your personal code, your ethics. We all have lines... lines we dare not cross, lines we think will break us... until we realize they won't, that life goes on, so we draw new ones."

And speaking of lines, the cruel lines of Murder Town come into view, all sharp angles and surreal, serrated architecture. The buildings look like knives, broken skulls, and other unpleasant things. Like everything in Tartarus, the place has a strange but terrible beauty, the kind you could get lost in and never leave.

There's a bridge ahead, a long stone bridge, but it never reaches the opposite shore. It's broken, leading nowhere but to a lengthy drop into the blood-water below. There are ghosts on the bridge, laughing ghosts, and for a moment, I think Murder Town might not be so bad. It looks like the laughing ghosts are fishing, but with rope—rope that ends in nooses. The ghosts cast them over the side, and I wonder how they will ever catch fish like that. Only they're not trying to catch fish.

They're trying to catch *people*.

Other ghosts, surely. The ghosts of their victims, who bob along in the crimson current screaming, gasping, and groaning.

"Got one!" a murderer cackles. He hauls up his line, dragging the victim from the bloody river below. Dragging her by the noose wrapped tight around her neck. "She's a live one," he exclaims. "Watch her kick!"

And she does, legs dancing on air, arms grasping at the noose. Her eyes bulge, her tongue lolls like a pink snake trying to escape the cave of her mouth. Her face purples, her beauty fades. The killers on the bridge laugh and congratulate their friend.

"You know the rules," one of the murderers says. "Catch and release. Save some for the rest of us!"

The victorious ghost grudgingly cuts his line, sending the strangled girl back into the bloody river. I watch her drift away, seemingly dead, and I wonder how that's possible, but then she comes back to life, screaming and moaning again.

*Begging to be killed.*

"It's all a game to them," Hannah says. "To those on the bridge, and those below."

"A sick game," I say, and can't believe I'm still watching. The scene has all the terrible fascination of a traffic accident, only it's never-ending. I'm reminded of the Ritual of the Worm in the temple back home... Where the priests hang a sinner from a blessed meathook, then hack off his legs and force him to crawl around the temple, praying for forgiveness. Crawling, like a worm. And if the sinner can't make a complete circuit of the temple, they cast him into the pit... a sacrifice to Cronus.

I've never liked the ritual, never much liked going to temple for that matter, but when you're raised to go, to watch, to never say or think or do anything contrary to the priests' teachings, well... This is what you get.

The New Greece Theocracy isn't a town full of murderers and victims. It's a country full of them, the last country on Earth. And once we defeat Cronus... once we stop the crazy rituals and the sacrifices, what then? What do we have left? What do we have that's worth saving?

I don't know, and that scares me. It fills me with unfathomable dread. Once the war is won, the real struggle, the struggle to rebuild our country and the soul of our people, begins...

The ghosts notice us watching and pause their game to wave, ghoulishly beckoning us to come join in. Each ghost wears the same mad, fixed smile, watching our every move with cold, cunning eyes. Even their victims join in, begging us not to help, but to join them...

One of the madmen on the bridge even hurls his noose at us. It's a good throw, good enough for the rope to land at my feet. I kick it into the river.

As we walk away, I can't help but feel we're walking into a noose of our own—one fastened by Cronus with Hades as the bait.

# 23

ALL YOUR EYES CAN SEE

HADES' SCENT leads us from the banks of Murder Town into open country. Here, the broken land looks like an open wound, the brittle, dusty ground shot through with clay—clay as red as blood.

I feel better with the ghost city and its ghastly fishermen behind us, even though I know where we're going will be worse. We're going right where Cronus wants us to, doing exactly what the King of the Titans wants us to do.

I'm more stressed than ever because as the Bridge Between Worlds, I have more power than ever. Power to decide who lives and who dies. It's power I never asked for, power I never wanted, and once the Olympians know I have it, they'll expect me to use it for them, the same way Cronus wants me to use it for him. I can only hide it so long, and then... I'll have to decide. But first, I have to figure out how to use my secret power, on top of whatever other powers I have. I haven't even mastered the ones I know, so how I'm supposed to wipe out a whole race of immortals, I don't know.

We come across the dried-out shell of a monstrous scorpion, a black-armored nightmare the size of a tank. Cerberus pauses to sniff at the husk, so we take the opportunity to rest. Hannah passes out water and energy bars, and we sit with our backs against the shell.

"Aren't you running low?" I ask, then notice something weird: her leather belt pouch is way too small to have held all the food and water she's been handing out.

She smiles and hands me the pouch. "Go on, open it."

The inside is pitch-black. I stick my hand in, but don't feel anything, including the bottom. "What the hell?" I mutter. I pull my hand out and turn the bag upside down. Nothing falls out when I shake it. "This some sort of trick?"

She grins impishly. "Well, I am a witch."

"So you keep saying."

"Check it out; that's the first real magic item I made. I needed something to hold all my stuff, since I was always on the move. It basically holds infinity of whatever. Mostly food and water, bird seed for Shadow, a few odds and ends."

"Then how come it's empty?"

"It's not, but you have to know what you want. If it's in there, you'll find it."

I stick my hand back in, and rummage around. I think about a bottle of water, and feel one slide into my hand. I pull my arm out, and there it is: a fresh bottle. "So it's like a magic vending machine?"

"Yeah, it's also a purse, a backpack, a whole damn storage unit. The only limitation is it only holds whatever fits in the opening."

"So no pillows, chairs, or tents, nothing like that?"

"I wish!" she says. "Anyway, if I wasn't always on the run, I'd have made all kinds of cool items by now."

I hand her the pouch. "It's great though. Really clever."

"Thanks." She opens the pouch and digs out some bird seed for Shadow. The familiar greedily pecks at the tasty kernels. "You know, as much as I like big flashy magic, I still prefer small, practical tricks like this. It's the little things that make life easier."

I shrug. "You might not think that way if you'd lived in a palace instead of by your wits."

"Oh, I spent some time in palaces too," Hannah says. "My father's castle, Mount Olympus... Right, cousin?" She nudges the War God in his ribs.

Ares gives her a grudging look. "You were always getting underfoot." He says it without malice, the faint trace of a smile crossing his face. "Not much of a princess at all."

My jaw drops. "What? You're a princess?"

She laughs. "Seriously? You didn't know? My father is the king. That makes me a princess; the princess of all your eyes can see..." She gestures good-naturedly at the desolate landscape, and I'm about to say something clever when her face changes, eyes growing wide in alarm. "We've got company!"

Ares is on his feet, sword out, before either of us can do anything. Shadow launches into the air. Cerberus growls, fur bristling. Hannah and I get up, drawing our blades.

There's a dust cloud on the horizon. A dust cloud caused by galloping horses. No, not horses. *Centaurs.*

"It's Captain Nessus," I say. "He's found us!"

## 24

THE CLIFFS OF PAIN

"They're still a ways off," I say. "I count two dozen centaurs. Can we outrun them?"

Ares shakes his head. "The terrain's too open and they're fast. If we make our stand here, we have cover. The giant scorpion shell prevents them from taking us from behind."

"OK, good." I look around, desperate for anything else that can help us. Then I remember I don't have to look for help, not when I can make my own. "I've got an idea..."

Ares raises an eyebrow. "Better make it a good one."

"It is... Remember in class when you taught us about tactics?"

Ares nods.

"Well, If I dig a couple of trenches with my magic, and make them wide enough the centaurs can't leap over, then we force them to come at us one at a time. Funnel them in—and onto our waiting blades."

"I see I trained you well," Ares says with a proud smile, melting some of the ice that's stood between us since last night.

A black smudge stains the air above the centaurs.

The War God sighs. "Harpies! Now the enemy can come at us from above. Still, a trench will help. You should get started—"

"Or we could ride Cerberus," Hannah interrupts.

Ares and I stare at her, then the monster dog.

"You mean all three of us?" I ask.

"Yep. He has three heads—that's three necks, one for each of us to hold onto. And he's fast. Aren't you, boy?"

Cerberus cocks his heads in triplicate.

She gives the nearest head a scratch on the cheek. "You can do it, can't you?"

Cerberus pants enthusiastically. It would be cute if he wasn't so damned ugly.

---

THE BIG DOG IS FAST, even carrying the three of us. She tells the beast to take us in the last known direction of Hades' scent.

"Won't he lose it?" I ask, struggling to cling to the creature's left head. "We're going awfully fast for him to track!"

"It's OK," Hannah says, clearly comfortable riding behind the center head. "If he loses it, he'll pick it up again when we outrun the enemy."

"*If* we outrun them," Ares says from behind the third head. "If you ask me, the bastards are keeping pace."

Hannah glances over her shoulder. "I know this dog. He can outrun any monster in the kingdom!"

The hound of Hades barks in agreement.

I've never taken a dog's word before, but in my crazy life, there's a first time for everything.

---

OUR LEAD WIDENS, the centaurs and harpies falling farther and farther behind. Everything seems to be going to plan until the horizon erupts into orange fire.

"What the hell is that?" I yell.

"The Phlegethon," Hannah answers. "The River of Flame!"

We're getting closer to Cronus, to the center of Tartarus. I can feel it, like a steel-clawed hand squeezing my heart. The air turns hot, smoky, my vision blurring against rising waves of heat.

"Can we jump it?" I ask.

"Too wide!" Hannah calls back. "There's a bridge..." She points west, then speaks into Cerberus' ear. The dog alters course, following the flaming river instead of heading toward it. There are black cliffs ahead, made from basalt, a type of volcanic rock. They look old and weathered, with the gigantic skulls of men and beasts carved into the surface.

"The Cliffs of Pain," Hannah explains. "This is where ghosts go to commit suicide. They jump off the bridge I told you about."

"And they die?" I ask.

Hannah shakes her head. "No, silly. They just go to sleep for a while. Then they wake up and jump again until they work out whatever's troubling them."

This place is insane, and I feel it driving me a little mad too. The more I'm down here, the more normal it seems... What happens when I accept this as my reality? What happens when I get back to Earth?

*Stop worrying about the future,* I scold myself, *or there might not be one.*

The parched ground climbs toward the cliffs, cutting off our view of the river. Then we're at the base.

Above, the gem-crusted ceiling shines, reflecting the eerie orange light of the Phlegethon snaking its way through the cavern floor. There's a couple hundred feet to the clifftop, and however many more to reach Hannah's bridge.

Up we go, the steep path getting narrower and narrower until it forces Cerberus to slow down or risk falling. Finally, the dog stops. The three thick-furred heads whine, and I can feel the sound vibrating through the flesh of his neck and into my bones.

"He wants us to get off," Hannah explains. "The path's too narrow and the extra weight makes him nervous."

We dismount, giving the dog a few reassuring pats. Below, the centaurs are almost to the bottom of the cliffs. They're big beasts, not as big as Cerberus, but they'll still be forced to come up single file—and tread carefully with their hooves.

"It's not the centaurs you should be worried about," Ares says. "It's the harpies."

He's right. I count fifteen of them. The grotesque bird-women swoop closer, shrieking and cackling.

"We'd better get ahead of Cerberus," Ares says. "We can move faster than him here."

We pick our way up the trail, hoping to reach the top before the harpies reach us, but it's a fool's hope. We're only halfway to our goal when the first harpy wings her way into battle. I start to draw my sword, then think better of it. The sword's not long enough. What I need is a missile weapon.

*What I need is a rock.*

I reach into the cliff, my fingers melting through the basalt like butter. With one fluid motion, I pull a chunk free and hurl it at the attacking harpy. It connects with her skull, smashing past the snapping beak. I hear the crunch of bone, the squish of brain, and then the bird-woman spirals to the ground a hundred feet below.

"Great shot!" Ares shouts, but Hannah warns, "Watch out! More coming!"

I tear a pair of stones free, one in each hand, and send two more harpies hurtling down. The remaining bird-women are more cautious now. They hover out of range and call for my blood.

## 25

THE POWER OF ME

"GET TO THE TOP!" I shout. "I'll hold them off."

"Don't let anything happen to Cerberus," Hannah warns. "We need him to find Hades."

"I won't! I promise."

The witch nods, flaring out her purple cloak. Her body turns to fog, floating straight up.

Ares gives me a confident nod, then races up the narrow trail after Hannah as fast as he can. I realize how much that nod means, and how rarely it must be given. The God of War just told me to "handle it." *He trusts me in a fight.* If that wasn't clear before, it is now, and it fills me with a sense of pride.

That leaves Cerberus. The dog-beast is behind me, and because he's so big, he can't maneuver that quickly or that well. He whines, wondering why we're not following the others.

"You go on, boy," I tell him. "I'll be right behind you!" I get out of the dog's way by digging my fingers into the cliff face and climbing up and around him.

I drop back to the path as a harpy dives toward the hound. I don't have time to grab a rock, so I aim my wrist at the devil-bird and one of the three crystal daggers magically embedded into my hand shoots out. The missile catches the harpy by surprise, punching through her feathered breast in a hot splash of gore.

That buys me time to pull another pair of rocks free from the cliff. Two more harpies are swooping in, but veer off when they see I'm armed again. I hurl the rocks anyway, missing one and clipping the other, but the damage isn't enough to drop her.

*Eleven harpies left.*

I stare at the advancing centaurs. The monstrous cavalry are coming up the path now. Captain Nessus isn't in the lead, nor are his brothers Democ and Ruvo, which is a shame. It's a shame because I want them to be. I want it to be them I try my latest idea on, but it can't wait.

After hurling a few more rocks to keep the harpies away, I tear a larger stone loose. It's the size of a small boulder, but I don't send it after the harpies. I send it rolling down the path to crash into the centaurs below.

*The centaurs who have no room to dodge.*

The boulder smashes through one, sends another spilling off the trail, then repeats the process a few more times before going over the cliff itself. The beast-men cry out in shock and horror, though this quickly turns to cries of rage. A pair of them try to race up, but I send another boulder hurtling down, taking the centaurs out.

*Sixteen centaurs left.*

Nessus hurls curses. I'm too high up to make out the words, but I'm sure they're creative. And speaking of creative... I kneel down and punch through the downward path. Cracks appear. I punch again. The black stone shatters, crumbling, creating a deadly gap for anyone attempting to climb from below.

I survey my handiwork, then step back and punch again to widen the gap. I plan to keep doing it until the gap is so wide no centaur can possibly leap it.

Unfortunately, the harpies don't like that. Before I can complete my plan, claws rake into my back, then fasten onto my shoulders, threatening to lift me up. I slam my left hand into the cliff wall to hang on, and reach back with the right. All I find is feathers. I can't get a grip.

"Carry you off!" the harpy croaks in her bird-like voice. "Break your bones! Break your bones!"

Now I'm sorry I only covered my chest and shoulders in crystal armor. I don't feel pain like humans do, but I feel the deep furrows in my back. I feel her talons pressing into my shoulders. The bird-woman's strength is fierce as she renews her grip, trying to yank me from the cliff. My feet slide along the dusty path, sending dirt and rocks scattering to the distant cavern floor.

Again, I flail with my free hand, this time taking hold of the harpy's elongated vulture-neck. I squeeze. She lets out a startled squawk. Her beak snaps hard in a violent peck that bounces off the side of my head. My vision swims, but I don't let go. Her greedy talons sink deeper into my shoulders, cracking the armor there. This isn't working. I can't get the right leverage to strangle her. Then I remember I'm gripping the harpy's neck with my right hand—my dagger hand.

With a thought, I let go and extend the two remaining daggers past my knuckles. I thrash my arm up in a savage half-punch, half-flail. It connects. Greasy monster gore spills down my arm. The claws in my back are gone. The harpy flaps away in a frightened arc, squirting black blood from her ruptured artery like one of my family's oil wells. She doesn't fly far before she goes limp, spiraling down to splat on the hard-baked floor.

*Ten harpies left.*

"Come on!" I dare the remaining bird-women. "Come on, you monsters, you devils! Take me if you can!" I point my dagger hand at them, seeking targets. The flock breaks formation, desperate to fly out of range.

I stand there, gasping, feeling the sticky wetness of my wounds. My back's bad, I can tell, but it's my head that worries me. It's bleeding a lot and a flap of scalp hangs loose. *That bitch tried to crack my skull like an egg.*

I glance up the path and see Cerberus climb over the top. He's safe. We're all safe. For now.

A sudden wave of dizziness washes over me, and I'm glad I have one hand rooted into the cliff wall, or I might have fallen. The contact with the stone feels good, it feels right. It sends new strength surging through me.

Instead of running up the cliff path, I climb the wall. Straight up, scuttling like a spider. I expect to be attacked, but the harpies have had enough of me. They fly over the clifftop seeking easier victims. Judging by the sounds of battle that follow, I'm guessing they don't find any.

As I climb, I remember the words I used to say in my dreams as I climbed Mount Olympus:

*I am the mountain.*

*I am one with it.*

*I am one with the earth.*

Saying the words gives me focus. They give me strength. Things are healing inside me, stitching shut, even as my power is breaking loose.

*The power of me, the power to be!*

There's no other feeling like it.

## 26

WAR IS HELL

WHEN I PULL MYSELF over the top, I see the cliff is more or less level now, extending for miles to the east and west but breaking up a few hundred feet north where the river cuts a molten path through its base. A matching set of cliffs stand further north, opposite the divide. The air up here is smoky, lit with occasional flurries of hot ash and cinder.

The battle is over. Cerberus shakes two harpies in the jaws of his left and right heads while the central one takes turns biting chunks out of both. Ares has sliced the heads off two more bird-women, and Hannah has stabbed another.

*Five harpies left.*

They fly overhead, throwing promises of hate and revenge. I look down, two hundred feet below, and see the centaurs have abandoned their attempt to climb the cliff's damaged trail.

"They're splitting up," I tell the Olympians. "The centaurs won't be coming up the cliff, I took care of that."

Ares flicks black blood from his golden blade. "They're trying to outflank us."

"Should we be worried?" I ask.

"That depends."

"On what?"

"On how many are left."

"Sixteen. Two groups of eight, one galloping east, the other west."

"This is your land. You know where they're going?" Ares asks Hannah.

Before the witch can answer, Cerberus succeeds in tearing the two harpies in half. Pink guts uncoil, plopping to the ground and writhing like snakes. The smell is horrible, the sight even worse because the harpies aren't dead... We turn away from the messy feast as the dog-monster gulps and chews the harpies' guts.

"Well, that was horrible," I say to no one in particular. "What's that old expression? 'War is hell'?"

Ares grunts with amusement then walks off to clean his blade.

Hannah smirks. "Welcome to Tartarus."

"Um, yeah. Thanks... Thanks a lot! I'm not going to be able to get that scene out of my head, am I?"

"Depends what else you see." She winks, but doesn't elaborate. "Anyway, back to the centaurs... You say they're headed east and west?"

"Yeah."

"Both directions lead to crossings further down, but they're miles away, so we shouldn't be seeing them for a while."

"They'll probably show up at the worst possible moment."

Hannah smirks. "Monsters always do. Looks like you took some wounds."

"Harpy got me." I gingerly touch the wound in my scalp and hiss at the pain.

"Bad?"

"I'm healing. That's why I went up the side instead of taking the path. Thought it'd be quicker—both the healing and the trip."

Hannah pulls a travel size medical kit out of her magic pouch. "Let me fix you up; things are only going to get tougher from here."

I wince as she ministers to my wounds. "Ow! Hey, take it easy, will ya?"

"I'm a witch, not a nurse," Hannah says. "Besides, you get what you pay for."

I hear a juicy popping sound, and against my better judgment, send my gaze in that direction. Hannah's familiar is pecking the eyes out of the harpies, doing a happy little raven dance as he gobbles the bloodshot morsels down.

I turn away, then groan as the sudden motion causes Hannah's hands to slip on my wound.

"Eyes front, soldier!" she teases. "The beasts have their hungers, and we have ours." She plants a surprise kiss on my lips. "You were brave back there. Very commanding."

"Yeah? You like that?"

"Uh-huh," she nods. "You're turning into a real hero. I knew you had it in you."

"You did?"

She shrugs. "Ares told me about you. Before, back on Earth. He's proud of you too. Has been for quite some time."

"That's good to know."

"Yes and no."

"Why? What's so bad about it?"

Hannah lowers her voice. "The more he respects you, the more he expects of you. And my cousin can be pretty demanding."

"And you can't?" I try to make it a joke, but there's some truth in it.

She gives my wound one last jab on purpose. "There! All done. You'll live."

"Yeah, but it's not like I have a choice."

"You will," she promises. "Soon."

# 27

## THE BRIDGE OF BURNT SOULS

"Suicide Bridge is about a mile this way," Hannah says, patting Cerberus on the rump. The big dog bounds forward, glad to have room to move.

"Why don't you send your familiar to scout ahead?"

Hannah points at the five harpies trailing us. "Because of them. Shadow's a tough old bird, but he's safer with me."

"Yeah, you're probably right. So... Suicide Bridge, huh? That's its name? Not very poetic compared to the Pillars of Ash, Garden of Bone, and all the other weird places you've taken me."

"Suicide Bridge is the slang name," Hannah explains. "Its formal name is 'The Bridge of Burnt Souls.' Why? You like that better?"

"No, not really... Hey, no offense, but your father's kingdom is pretty morbid."

She gives me one of her trademark snorts. "At least it's consistent. Earth is all over the place in its naming conventions—or at least it was, before the Gods War."

"So about the war," I ask, "I'm curious... I know what the Theocracy taught me, but I never really got the Olympians' side of the story."

Ares gives me a pained look. "You want our side? Zeus should have killed Cronus and the rest of the Titans when he had the chance! But he thought imprisoning them—like how he'd been imprisoned in Cronus' stomach—would make them suffer more. He wanted to look down at them, trapped in the ice, and gloat. With the Titans as his prisoner, Zeus could show how powerful he was, could always have some trophy to point to."

"It was a mistake," Hannah says.

Ares fumes. "It was more than a mistake! It was stupid! And his ego, his vanity, got him killed, and put the rest of us in a world of hurt. Let me give you a little advice, Andrus: If you have the chance to kill your enemy, do it. Don't play games or try diplomacy. Don't gloat. *Just kill and kill, and kill again!* That's how you end a war, and that's how you prevent the next one."

"But wouldn't that put you out of a job?" I ask.

Ares glares at me, but then claps me on the back and roars laughter instead. "Oh-ho! I like you, Andrus. You're all right!"

"For a Titan?" I add.

"Yes," he says, "definitely for a Titan."

"You didn't ask me how I handled the enemy back on the cliff."

"Do I need to? You're here, and the centaurs aren't. That tells me all I need to know. You've come a long way."

"For a Titan?"

"No," he says with a smile. "For my student."

We walk on for a bit before Hannah holds up a hand to stop us. "Guys, I hate to interrupt your male bonding, but we're here…" She points past Cerberus to a black bridge, two hundred feet long and fifty feet wide.

The Bridge of Burnt Souls is made of stone carved from the same basalt as the cliffs. It was likely always part of them rather than added later, though it's certainly been refined since then. Like the cliff walls, the bridge's guard rails are carved with skulls, only there's something different about these. They're not carvings at all, but real skulls—entire skeletons—burnt into the rock walls of the bridge as decoration. Melted men, women, and children, mouths open, forever fused in agony.

Far below simmers the molten current of the Phlegethon. Hot clouds of ash shot through with cinders blow up from the River of Flame and across the bridge. There are no ghosts here, no lost souls looking to commit spiritual suicide.

There's something worse... A massive shadow that lurks on the other side. A fifty-foot shadow that steps out of the swirling clouds and into the orange hell-light.

Gyges the Reaver, Gyges the Invincible. The Destroyer. He of the Hundred Hands Who Guards the Gate, and now this Bridge. The Lesser Titan stops halfway across, his fifty heads set in expressions of hate and hunger. "Little brother!" he bellows. "Now you are here. Now, we shall fight!"

# 28

## NO FUTURE WITHOUT A FIGHT

I DON'T THINK ANYTHING ever prepares you to face a nightmare. You'd think familiarity would—it's not like I haven't seen Gyges before, talked to him, gotten a feel for what the giant is capable of. But I haven't really fought him, Ares has. And I had run. It was true the War God had told me to, but I had been glad to flee that fight. I'm no coward, but I'm no fool either.

Gyges is a mountain. A mountain of mouths and muscle, and so ugly, so savage, it hurts to look at him. It hurts even more to know he is my brother, a Titan like me, yet not like me.

The fifty hungry heads... forty-nine of men and beasts and mixtures of the two... and the one in his belly, the giant fanged "O" of leech-like horror ringed by spider eyes, black eyes, multifaceted and glittering in the firelight like gems. There is no sign of the damage I saw Ares inflict, except for the eye he kicked in, but even that has scabbed over.

His hundred arms either bear weapons or are weapons, every-thing from tentacles to crab claws. And his feet are weapons too, monstrous eagle talons. Some of the weapons he carries in his human-like hands are boulders, some whale bones fashioned into clubs or sharpened into axes.

I don't want to fight Gyges, but I can't run. There's nowhere to run to.

"Last time," the giant scolds me, "you cheated! You ran, like a coward, and let the War God fight your battle."

"I also talked," I tell him. "I tried to get you to side with me, against Cronus."

Gyges laughs. "And I told you, there is no future without a fight! So now you fight me, little brother. You fight and win, then we talk. You fight and lose..."—he shrugs his massive shoulders—"Nothing left to talk about!"

"You've got a point," I say, trying desperately to think of some plan to stall or defeat him. "I shouldn't have run before."

The giant grunts. "I understand why you did... Gyges the Mighty! Gyges the Invincible!" At that, his other forty-nine heads snarl and roar. "Everyone runs from me, or tries. Even your little God ran in the end."

Ares takes a threatening step forward, drawing his magic blade, then checks himself. "This is your fight," he says. "If you can defeat him, you can defeat any of the Titans."

"Even Cronus?"

"You might need a little help with that," Hannah says.

I nod and walk to the bridge. Gyges' animal heads drool and gnash their teeth in anticipation. "I'll fight you, brother, but on one condition: Let my friends pass."

"Friends?" Gyges growls. "Friends! You call those things friends? They are traitors! The bad dream of our people. Why should I let them pass?"

"Because you don't want them to interfere in the fight, and because Cronus wants to see what I can do on my own."

Gyges narrows his eyes, but makes no reply.

"Let the Olympians pass, then we'll have a fair fight, you and I."

"A fair fight?" The idea seems to both amuse and delight the giant. "You think fighting me will be fair?"

"As fair as it gets: Titan against Titan. There is honor in that, brother. Honor and glory!"

"Now you speak the language of the brave, the true Titan! This pleases me. This pleases your father."

"So you'll let them go? I can make them promise not to interfere."

"No!" Gyges snarls. "Gods have lied to me before. Gods always lie! I have many ears, but none that hear such treachery."

"What if they promise me instead?"

"Andrus," Hannah says, "you don't have to do this..."

"Yes, I do. It's OK. Freeing your father is what's most important. I want you to promise me you won't interfere. You and Ares both. *Swear it.* Swear it and keep your vow, no matter what happens."

The God of War gives me a stern look. "What did I just tell you about diplomacy?"

"I know. I have to try."

"Very well, it's your decision. This is where your life has led you, and where it ends or begins. Nothing can change that now. Remember your training... and go for the eyes in his stomach. That's his weak spot."

"I'll remember."

"Andrus," Hannah tries again. "Be reasonable! We can take him together."

"No, I can do this... at least, I think I can. And if I can't, how much good can I be to you later, when things get really tough?"

"A lot of good," she insists, "but I'll swear."

And they do, loud enough for Gyges to hear. They swear by Zeus and Hades and everything they hold dear.

"Well?" I call to the giant. "Does that satisfy you?"

"Nothing from Olympus satisfies me," Gyges sneers. "The question is, does it satisfy you?"

"It does."

"Then it is on your head when the Gods break their promise! It stains your honor, not mine, and forever robs you of your glory if you defeat me."

"You mean *when* I defeat you."

Gyges laughs. "Such spirit, little brother! Tell the scum to pass... Pass me if they dare!" The giant steps sideways and mock-bows, gesturing with fifty of his hands for my friends to walk by, free from harm.

Before she goes, Hannah tries to hand me her magic cloak. "For luck," she whispers.

"You mean in case I lose. No, Hannah, I can't accept it. Not this time. This fight... it has to be fair. It has to be to the end. One way or another."

Reluctantly, Hannah refastens the cloak around her shoulders. "You're an idiot," she says, then kisses me hard on the mouth. "A beautiful idiot! Maybe that's what I love about you." Before I can think of a clever response, she follows Ares, calling for Cerberus and Shadow to join them.

"See you soon!" Gyges taunts the Olympians as they pass him on the bridge. The giant and I both watch until they are safely on the other side, then Gyges turns to me with an enthusiastic growl.

My friends stand at the opposite end, but I wave them off. "Go!" I shout. "Don't wait for me!"

They move off, disappearing behind a curtain of smoke. From above and behind me comes the furious flapping of wings as the remaining harpies shoot overhead, racing across the bridge in pursuit.

I have no idea how I'm going to beat Gyges, I just know I have to. I do some stretches, both to prepare my body and buy my friends some time. I have no idea how long this fight is going to last, and if I lose, I want them to get as far away from here as possible.

The giant waits on the bridge, watching me with hungry amusement. "Is it fear that delays you, little brother?"

"No, I just want to give you the best fight I can. That is what you want, isn't it? What Cronus wants?"

Gyges nods, the casual motion of so many heads moving in unison is as disconcerting as anything the giant does. "I will tell the story of how I defeated the son of Cronus many times! I will tell of your doom to my children, and my children's children. I will tell it to the winds, and the rain, the smoke, and the fire! All shall know it was

Gyges who crushed you this day on the Bridge of Burnt Souls. A glorious victory for me, a glorious fate for you!"

I'm as ready as I'll ever be. I draw my sword—glad I have one of Ares' golden blades—and step onto the bridge. The fused skeletons in the guard rails are even more gruesome in closeup, and I hope I won't end up like them, or worse.

Gyges stomps a taloned foot impatiently, then gestures me to come at him. "Come, little brother! Come to Gyges! Come to your doom..."

# 29

## TITAN AGAINST TITAN

I CHARGE.

Gyges is fast. He hurls boulders at me. I dodge one, slice through another, and use my free hand to reach out to a third with my magic. The boulder is slapped aside as if it weighed no more than a paperweight. It sails over the side of the bridge, becoming a distant splash in the lava below. I'm stunned I did it, but I don't have time to dwell on my success. Gyges sends more boulders my way. Again, I dodge. Again, I slice, and slap another aside.

Gyges roars and hurls the last boulder at me. It's a big one, the biggest yet, and he hurls it with perfect accuracy. It can't be dodged. Slicing seems risky; I've never tried to chop through anything this bulky before, and besides, I've got a better idea. I'm going to try something new. I'm going to turn his own weapon against him.

Summoning all my will, I reach out to the rushing rock. I reach out with my magic, my courage, my birthright as the son of Cronus, the son of Gaia. I reach out with everything, everything I have and everything I imagine I have.

*I am the mountain.*

*The mountain is me.*

*Together, we fight!*

The boulder slows, the boulder stops, and I hold it there a moment, suspended in mid-air while I work up its momentum again. Spinning it, building up force, energy.

When I release it, I send it snapping back at the giant with all my anger, all my hatred. It tumbles with the rage of loss, the fury of the righteous. And it strikes Gyges, plowing into him, pulping at least a dozen of his fifty heads in a violent fountain.

Gyges screams, staggers back, then falls, thrashing in pain. The bridge shakes. *The bridge cracks.* A hot wind blows up from the river below. I'd meant to hit his chest dead center, but Gyges ducked—he just didn't duck far enough.

I have to keep moving. I need to press my advantage while I still can. I race toward the thrashing giant, and as I do, I leap onto the railing. I get a terrifying glimpse of the molten river below, then focus my full attention on the giant.

Gyges is struggling to rise, his bent and broken heads flopping grotesquely. But it's not them I care about. It's the central face, the leech-like horror in his belly with the spider eyes. I'm aiming for that. That's why I'm running along the wide stone railing, trying to get enough height so that when I jump, I can reach my target.

*Go for the eyes,* Ares told me. *Go for his weak spot.*

I jump. Sword raised in both hands, blade pointed down. Gyges is getting up fast, so I miss the top ring of eyes and have to settle for the ones below. My blade strikes home, my blade strikes true. The black eye pops, bursting like an overripe grape. Again Gyges screams, and again I jump, this time away from the giant.

I hit the stone bridge and roll. Just like gym class. Just like Mr. Cross taught me, but my victory is short-lived. A tentacle slams down, coiling around me with bone-crushing force, the grip of a python. I'm lifted up. Ten, twenty feet off the ground, then thirty, then it doesn't matter because a crab claw is coming at me, pincers snapping like a madman's scissors.

I have one arm free. My sword arm. I swing the glowing blade down, hacking through the tentacle's rubbery flesh. I'm falling then, but timed so the pincers snap shut on empty air.

I drop to the bridge, losing my sword in the process. It goes skittering away, glowing gold, and I'm scrambling after it when another tentacle slips around my ankles. This time, I have both hands free, but no blade, and I'm hanging upside down, all the blood rushing to my head, all the adrenalized horror pumping through me as Gyges lifts me toward his leech mouth. Rows and rows of needle-like fangs gleam between purple gums, and the stench of rotten meat wafts past them.

I extend the crystal daggers from my right hand and aim for one of the spider eyes. *Mother Gaia, guide my hand!* I fire the missile, and am rewarded by the sickly wet pop of bursting eye-juice, then by being let go. Unfortunately, not dropped. Hurled. Hurled hard, hurled fast. I'm going over the guard rail. Into the the River of Flame...

I have one chance, and that's to grab onto the railing. It's a close call. Very close, but I manage to hold on. I hang there, the wind knocked out of me, the magma below boiling and churning as if calling me to join it...

Gyges is hurt, he's crashing around, bellowing, lashing out in all directions. He had eight working spider eyes before Ares took one in the Garden of Bone. Now I've taken another, but I only have one crystal dagger left. More cracks appear in the stonework. I pull myself up and haul my aching body over the railing, back onto the bridge.

Gyges sees me and charges, giant eagle legs pumping, talons scratching furrows in the bridge floor.

I see my sword, just a few feet away. I see the bridge rail, and make my decision. I rip a chunk out of the railing and send it skittering across the bridge floor, directly in Gyges' path. The Lesser Titan trips over it, and in his wounded condition, stumbles and falls.

I'm already in motion, picking up the golden blade, and running toward Gyges, then leaping up onto him, chopping through the hairy head of a wild boar, dodging the fangs of a snake head, then I'm on his back. It's a struggle to stay moving because Gyges is moving too. He's twisting around, trying to get at me with fifty feet of fury. Fifty feet of primordial rage.

Claws click.

Tentacles writhe.

I do my damage, ripping into his hairy back, plunging the sword in, plunging it deep and riding the buried blade down the same way Ares did. I push out when I hit his hip, somersaulting to the bridge below.

A bone axe whizzes toward me.

A club crushes down.

Rather than crippling the giant, I've only made him angrier. There's too much going on, too many hands or things that pass for hands. Too much everything, and all the time, the horrible sounds, the shrieks and shouts from dozens of heads.

My crystal armor takes a glancing blow—an axe blow that knocks me back but not out of the fight. The armor kept the edge away, but only blunted some of the force. I can't let him hit me again.

I lash out with my sword where I can, and leap away when I can't. Fighting Gyges isn't easy, even with all my power. Not that I thought it would be, but some brave, reckless part of me—the boy, not the man —thought I might have won by now. A glorious victory, and proof I have what it takes to beat Cronus.

We fight in a clash of wrath, Titan against Titan, knowing there can be only one. The good news is I'm able to get by him, so I head to the far end of the bridge. I want to be sure I'm on the right side if this thing crumbles... But why should it be 'if' since I can make it 'when'? Why not use my magic to crumble the bridge myself?

Gyges thunders after me. I whirl, drop to one knee and point my fist at the charging giant. One crystal dagger left. *Make it count!* I fire. Watch it punch through a spider-eye. Gyges screams. The wound slows him, and I use those precious seconds to slam my fists down on the bridge.

*I am the maker of mountains and the breaker of stones!*

The bridge shatters. Gyges falls. He falls into the Phlegethon, sinking below the fiery ooze and out of sight.

I watch the river, waiting to see if the giant surfaces, but he never does. I'm glad he's gone, glad I won, but there is sadness in my victory.

However monstrous Gyges was, however alien or evil, he was still my brother. I mourn his loss and what might have been.

A new rage rises in me, a red anger at the way the world is, the way it's always been, pitting brother against brother. Father against son.

"Are you watching, Cronus?" I yell. "Are you happy?"

The King of the Titans makes no reply. I am left with nothing—nothing but smoke and ruin. The way back is gone; the way forward filled with doubt.

## 30

---

### NO EASY ANSWERS

WALKING IN TARTARUS ALONE is different from being with friends. The last time it happened, I'd been pursued and hadn't had time to think. Now I do. I think back on my life, my present, my future. They stretch before and behind me, cast like shadows on the ground.

I've come down the other side of the Cliffs of Pain into a low valley. I'm within sight of the Phlegethon, the boiling current smoking along as it must have for millions of years.

I witness a group of penitent ghosts lining up by the river bank. Unmindful of the heat, they disrobe and wade into the lava. Some submerge themselves completely, others kneel, some squat, and some stand at various depths. Some scream, some cry, while others pray, and some say nothing at all as they burn and burn...

I've heard about this before, in one of those rare times I wasn't daydreaming in Mrs. Ploddin's history class... These ghosts are suffering, each according to their "sins" by how far they submerge their bodies. I'm not sure how much is punishment and how much is spiritual cleansing, and I don't stop to ask. The crazy thing is no one is forcing them into the lava; they're doing it to themselves.

It's a choice. A choice we all have without even realizing it.

*How many sins have I committed?*

Abandoning my family and Lucy? *Check.* Cheating on her with Hannah? *Check.* Fratricide? *Check,* now that Gyges is gone. Soon, I'll add patricide to the list. If I can find Cronus, and if I can kill him.

'Some things are forever,' Gyges had warned me. 'Some things are not. Who are you to say which is which?'

*Who am I?*

That's a good question. Before I found out I was a Titan, I worried I was a monster. Now I worry if I'm a hero. Is it all just a point of view? There are no easy answers. There's only me—here, now.

Alone.

---

I'VE BEEN FOLLOWING CERBERUS' TRACKS for about a mile when I come across the bodies of two of the five harpies that had flown in pursuit of my friends. They're not dead, of course; nothing can ever die completely while Hades is imprisoned. Instead, the bird-women lie in bloody, broken heaps. Still twitching. Forever twitching, wishing they were dead, yet knowing they will never find release, never fly again or find an end to their torment.

I step around them, and as horrible as they are, I almost wish I could put them out of their misery. One of the harpies snaps her beak at me, the other just glares, neck bent at an impossible angle. The ground is littered with black blood and feathers.

"I'm sorry," I tell the harpies. "It will all be over soon... For you, and for all the others caught between life and death."

They don't thank me, and I'm not sure they would if they could. But I know they'll be grateful when the pain stops. I know a lot of people will.

# 31

TOO FAR TO TURN BACK

I FIND MY FRIENDS a few miles later. They're standing at the edge of a flaming moat—a moat that surrounds a volcanic island. The lava snakes off and away, back toward the cliffs, a tributary to the River of Flame.

Two things stop me dead in my tracks: One, Cerberus is drinking from the moat, lapping lava like it was water. Second, the last three harpies are diving to attack. I open my mouth to shout a warning, but there's no need.

Cerberus raises his shaggy heads and breathes triple cones of fire. The bird-women become skyborne torches. Two of them plunge wildly into the moat, while the third lands near the dog's feet. Cerberus' heads fight over the flaming morsel, snapping and biting.

"I didn't know he could do that!" I say, half in surprise, half to announce my presence.

Ares and Hannah turn to face me. The witch runs and takes me in her arms, kissing me before I even have a chance to react. I find myself falling into it, matching her heat despite my guilt, despite my gloom. It all falls away in her arms, and I dare to hope again, to dream everything will work out.

"Andrus, you made it!" she says, then hugs me again.

"Was there ever any doubt?"

Ares walks up. "Not by me. Look at you! My star student."

"And Gyges?" Hannah asks.

"I dropped him off the bridge. I also dropped the bridge, so I hope there's another way back to the Styx."

"We'll think of something," Hannah says. "Let's not worry about that now."

I point to the island. "Is that it? Is that where Cronus has your father?"

"Cerberus thinks so. He picked up the scent again and the trail ends here."

"Her familiar's scouting the island," Ares says. "Should be back any minute. In the meantime, tell us about your victory. Don't leave anything out."

I recount the battle as best I can, though I take care to leave out the mixed feelings I had at the end. I do this for them as much as for myself.

"Glorious!" Ares exclaims when I'm done. "I told you, the eyes were the weak spot. Too bad you couldn't pop them all and blind that bastard."

"I popped enough."

"So you did. Well done! Your powers are growing."

"And your control," Hannah adds. "Power without control is... well, less than ideal." In a rush of wings, Shadow lands on her shoulder and squawks his report. The bird seems agitated. That's confirmed a few seconds later when Hannah translates, "The entire island is warded; it's the same kind of magic we faced in the Garden of Bone."

"So?" I say. "That's good news."

"Good news how?" she demands.

"Because that must mean this is the place, right? Besides, we beat this kind of magic before... That antipathy/sympathy thing."

"This is stronger," Hannah says. "The kind of magic needed to hold Cerberus is not the same strength as that needed to contain a God, particularly one as powerful as my father."

"So I'll break through the ward, just like last time."

"Andrus, it's not that simple..."

"Sure it is," I insist. "I'll just tunnel under the moat to get us over there, then break through the wards. Easy!"

"You'd have to tunnel pretty deep," Hannah says.

"Because of the lava? Good point. We wouldn't want that falling on our heads and flooding the tunnel. Can you fog up and fly over?"

"I wish, but the wards prevent that. I mean, I can fly over it, but can't land. That's the same problem Shadow had."

I nod. "All right, then let's tunnel. We've come too far to turn back now."

Hannah bites her lip. "Getting over there is one thing, getting inside..."

"It's OK," Ares says quickly. "Hannah, if Andrus says he can do it, he can. He hasn't let us down yet, and he won't let us down now."

I turn on my most confident smile. "You'll see. I got this!"

Ares casts a warning gaze over my shoulder. "We've also got something else."

I turn to see twin dust clouds on the horizon, coming from east and west. The centaurs have found us.

# 32

SACRIFICE

CERBERUS PADS UP AND DOWN the banks of the moat, pausing only for each head to take another drink of lava. Refueling his breath weapon. He'll need it. We'll all need it, and I'm glad he has it.

The centaurs are minutes away.

"You want me to start digging?" I ask. "Or are we making a last stand here?"

"No cover," Ares says. "No terrain advantage, except the moat prevents them from attacking us from behind."

"Not much of an advantage if they push us into it," Hannah mutters.

"True," I say. "Let me get a feel for the land before I start digging; I don't want to miscalculate."

Hannah nods.

"Sixteen centaurs," Ares muses, counting the enemy. "If I had my old vessel, I might have taken them."

"Yeah, well, you've got this one," I tell him. "You've got Mark, and you promised to take care of him, remember? No heroics."

"You mean no unnecessary ones," Ares corrects me.

Hannah rests a slim hand on my shoulder. "He's right, Andrus. We can't hesitate to sacrifice any of us when the time comes..."

I shrug her away. "Nobody's sacrificing anything! I'm going to get us to that island, we're going to free Hades, and we're all going to live happily ever after." I step away from the moat, back to what I feel is a safe distance. I close my eyes and reach out to the land, to Gaia, and into the future.

*You want me to be the Bridge,* I pray to her, *so please, Mother, let it start here.*

There is no voice from on high or deep below, just a gradual tingle, a slow-spreading shiver as my consciousness flows down through my body, through my feet, into the rock. It feels weird, yet feels so right. I see myself as not just inside the rock, but one with it. I see the perfect spot to dig, the perfect depth. But that will take too long, and besides, I have a better idea.

More dangerous, but ultimately more satisfying—if it works.

I kneel down and dig, hands scooping, shifting rock like child's toys. It's a good start. I widen the entrance. I widen it so it's large enough to fit Cerberus, which also means it's large enough to fit centaurs...

I'm dimly aware of the enemy's thundering hooves, more through the vibration than the sound, and far away, I hear something that sounds like "Hurry up!" in a sharp female voice. *Hannah.* The thought of her, the thought of everyone and everything at stake spurs me on to dig faster, drive harder, blending, blurring my way forward.

The tunnel widens, lengthening down, beneath the moat, into the earth and through it. I have to pause to get my bearings a few times, to adjust my course, my depth. This isn't a perfect tunnel, but it's perfect for the purpose I've built it for, and in the time that I have, with the skills that I have.

*The gifts, the talent.*

I'm aware I'm not alone now. I sense my friends are with me. And by the increasing power of the vibrations, I know the centaurs are here now too. When the vibrations stop, I know they are at the mouth of the tunnel. Debating about whether or not to follow us in.

I keep digging, digging like mad because I know the time is short. The time is now. Everything, everything is riding on this trap

I've made. When I sense the the centaurs are in, when I know they're far enough along—and more importantly, I know we are—that's when I build a wall behind us. That's when I build a wall, and once I'm sure it's strong, that's when I collapse the roof of the tunnel behind us.

Screams, screams, centaur screams baking in the heat.

And then another type of scream joins them, the screams of my friends, warning me the wall I built wasn't strong enough, and now there are cracks in it. Cracks like a dam. Cracks that ooze, cracks that melt, and I have a choice: I can either try to reinforce the wall, or I can keep tunneling forward.

I keep going.

*Don't stop. Never stop.*

Up, into the light. Up, out of danger!

We burst out of the tunnel, onto the dismal black rock of the island. We burst out, and behind us, from out of the tunnel, spews a geyser of pure liquid hell. The oil of the underworld. It fountains into the air, then rains down on us, as I desperately try to seal the breached tunnel.

Hannah works some kind of spell, shrouding us in an invisible shield of protective force. The lava splashes against that, then, when I yell it's safe, the fountain subsides and Hannah lets her spell go.

"You getting sloppy?" Hannah asks angrily. "Or did you plan that?"

I shrug. "It got us here, didn't it? And it got rid of the centaurs. Two-for-one." Only when I look to the far shore, I see I didn't get all the centaurs, only ten. Captain Nessus is still there, along with his brothers, Democ and Ruvo, and three others. They don't look happy, though it's hard to make out details at this distance. I let my imagination fill in the looks on their faces, the curses on their lips.

I wave to Nessus, and when I'm sure he's watching, give him the finger. "Next time," I promise. "Next time we meet, I'll kill you, because next time, you'll be able to die." I turn back to my friends. "OK, we're here. Now what?"

Hannah look around the desolate island. "The cell must be

underground. You couldn't have gotten us to it like you did with Cerberus?"

"I was in a hurry."

Her expression softens. "Right, sorry."

"I need a minute to recharge, but after that, I can start digging around. Or maybe Cerberus can sniff out the right spot?"

Hannah whispers something in the beast's ear, and it plods off, nose to the ground. "Now we wait."

I stretch my weary body and lay down on the rocks, closing my eyes and feeling one with the stone. "The adventure's almost over," I say. "What do we do next?"

"Whatever it takes," Ares says.

I open my eyes to stare at the War God. He seems deadly serious, even more than usual, but I decide to ignore it. It's just tough talk, the kind you expect from a guy like that. I shut my eyes and let myself drift, flicking through memories of happier times.

Were it not for the accident of my birth, I'd be a warrior now, proudly serving the New Greece Theocracy. Doing my duty. And then, after my military service was up, I'd join my father—foster father—at Eaves Oil. I'd be an executive. A rich playboy, though I've never been much for parties or people. And, let's face it, I've been hopeless with girls. I'd never found any that understood me until Mark's sister. Lucy, who had sacrificed herself to make sure Mark and I escaped. Lucy, who made all this possible.

Well, not just her... there's Hannah too. Hannah the witch, she of the dark hair and even darker eyes... We make sense together, don't we? Maybe we do, maybe we don't.

Maybe nothing makes sense, and we only fool ourselves into thinking things do. People, places, powers... I'm seventeen, standing on the bridge between the boy I was and the man I'll become. No, not the man. *The Titan.* And I'm not just standing on the bridge, *I am the bridge.* The Bridge Between Worlds, and I'm about to cross it. We all are. What waits on the other side?

"The prison," Hannah says, interrupting my thoughts. "Cerberus found it."

# 33

---

## FAMILY IS HARD

HADES' PRISON is in the center of the island. We trudge across the rocky surface, each step bringing us closer to the end of our quest. Cerberus barks excitedly, eager to be reunited with his master. Hannah has a similar sense of eagerness, one Ares doesn't seem to share. The War God looks what? Not angry, not sad. Resigned.

"Everything all right?" I ask him.

"It will be," the brooding God replies. "Soon."

"I always get worked up before a big event," I say, trying to lift his spirits. "Really pumped, you know? But after—or even near the end, when I feel it's slipping away—it gets hard."

Ares grunts.

We keep walking, hanging back now as Hannah and Shadow surge ahead to join Cerberus.

"It's not always getting lost in daydreams or the next event that spoil the end for me," I say.

"No?" Ares replies.

"No. Sometimes, it's just the enormity of the thing I've done, how hard I fought to be there, in that moment. And then I see it all slipping away, and I can't hold on, can't change or stop it from being over."

"The heat of battle," Ares agrees.

"Yeah, though it's not always a fight."

"Isn't it? Isn't everything in life a fight, Andrus? The struggle to be recognized..."

"By who?"

"By yourself, by others, by... family."

"Family is hard. Especially family like ours."

Ares nods. "My father, Zeus, was a hard man to love. My mother, Hera, was even worse."

"I've heard stories."

"Hearing isn't the same as living them," the War God says. "Trust me on that."

"At least your father wasn't Cronus."

Ares snorts. "There is that, but at least with Cronus, you know what to expect. As a Sky God, my father was... capricious. A tyrant one minute, generous and loving the next. I never knew how to please him."

"You did," I say. "I'm sure of it."

Ares stops, and I stop with him.

"What is it?"

"I want to tell you something, Andrus. Something important. I may not get another chance, and you deserve to hear it."

From fifty feet away, Hannah waves at us. "Hey, you two! What's the hold up?"

"Nothing," Ares calls back. "The boy needs a pep talk!"

Hannah shakes her head and I can't see it, but I can imagine the eye roll she must be giving us.

Ares says, "Did you know that Gods take on the quality of their portfolio?"

"What's that?"

"The things we represent. For example, my portfolio is War, Security, Virility, Revenge. Each is a different aspect of my godhood."

"So when you split into avatars, there were four of them, one for each aspect?"

"Correct."

"And the other three are dead?"

He nods.

"So which one are you?"

"I am War, first and last of my powers. But War is not just the glory and terror of battle, it is also change. Change and sacrifice."

"So is Death."

"Yes, in its own way. The difference is passion, of course, and duration. War requires passion, but the change can be fleeting. Death, however... Death is cold, passionless, permanent. It requires logic, the long view. I was never great at that."

"You're great at a lot of things."

"I was always a disappointment," Ares says, as if my praise doesn't matter. "A disappointment to my father, to my uncles—Poseidon and Hades—to my brothers and sisters, and all the rest. And why not? In the end, I disappointed them all. I couldn't save them! I could barely save myself."

"But you saved Hannah! You saved me. And you're still here."

"I'm still here," Ares agrees. "For now." He stares across the rocks to Hannah and Cerberus. The beast is pawing at the rocky ceiling of his master's prison. Scratching to get in, to wake Death after its long sleep. Ares turns his gaze back to me. "You're probably wondering why I'm telling you this."

"Well, yeah. Kind of."

"I have my reasons—not that I need any. I'm still a God, even reduced to being an avatar." He looks down at his hands—Mark's hands, the hands of a priest and scholar—and Ares seems lost in thought. Just when I'm about to ask what his reasons are, he continues. "I want you to understand something: You either control your portfolio, or it controls you. It's easy to lose yourself in your powers. It's also easy to lose yourself in your experiences, to let them drive your decisions. Like my father, and like yours."

"You're saying don't become like Cronus."

"Yes, but you have a mother too."

"Gaia? What's wrong with her?"

Ares shrugs. "We should join the others. No matter what

happens, I want you to know it has been an honor to be your teacher."

"And my friend."

Some fierce emotion passes over his face, there like a storm, then it's gone. "War doesn't have friends, Andrus. War has allies." And with that, the God walks away.

# 34

## HARD LESSONS

I'M LEFT STANDING THERE. Speechless. Ares opening up to me like that was unexpected and out of character. Not that I really know him that well. He's a complicated guy—God, whatever—and I suppose the pressure is getting to him.

I walk over to the group. Shadow circles overhead. The rest of the sky is clear. No harpies. Across the moat, the centaurs gallop away. Nessus knows he's lost, and sticking around now will only get him and his brothers killed.

Speaking of killing, I can't wait to get back to Earth and kill Inquisitor Anton. After that, after I've avenged Lucy, maybe I'll work my way up the Theocracy food chain, all the way to its high priest, Archieréas Enoch Vola himself. It will be weird being back on Earth after this trip. Part of me is desperate to go back, yet part of me wouldn't mind staying here, with Hannah. At least for a little while. There's something liberating about Tartarus. I don't have to hide who I am or what I can do. On Earth, even an Earth without the NGT, I don't think I could ever be myself like I can be here.

*Not if I want to walk among mortals.*

And I do, don't I? I do want to go back and make Earth better. But after that, then what? Cronus mentioned new worlds. New worlds—

not to conquer, but to explore. If I'm the bridge to them, then I could have endless adventures. I'd never have to stop being the hero. And that's the trick—to just keep going, never putting down roots, never trying to rule. Maybe that's where Cronus and Zeus and all the rest went wrong...

"You done daydreaming?" Ares asks.

"What? Oh, ha ha! Yeah, sorry. Old habits."

Hannah sighs. "OK, if you two are done male bonding, can we please get back to work? We don't know when Cronus is going to send more monsters."

"He won't," I say with more confidence than I should.

"Why not?"

"He wants us to free Hades, remember? It's all a game to him, and a test for me."

Hannah snorts. "Fine, then this is your final exam, Rock Boy. Make it good, my dad's waiting. I'll have Shadow keep an eye out, just in case you're wrong."

"When have I ever been wrong? Wait, don't answer that." I kneel down, examining the rocky center of the island.

"Well?" Hannah prompts.

"Gimme a second, I have to attune myself to the land."

"Well, can't you do it faster? Or do you need me to slap you?"

"No, you'd like it too much. And I meant 'gimme a second in silence.' I need to concentrate..." I reach out with my mind, becoming one with the rock, with the frozen heat of the long-dead volcano that made it. Working my way down, working until I feel the prison. "It's there," I tell the Olympians as I come out of my trance. "Same kind of warded stone cage as last time, but you're right. There's something about the wards... something different."

Hannah and Ares exchange a look.

"Can you do it? Can you move the rock out of the way?" Hannah asks. She crowds forward, voice trembling with eagerness.

"Yeah, no sweat. There's a lot of it though. Cronus buried your dad deep, a lot deeper than Cerberus."

Hannah kneels down so we're at eye level. She reaches out to cradle my face with both hands, pulling me close with her eyes, her lips, her voice. "Thank you for this, Andrus. You'll never know how grateful I am."

"Try me."

She does, brushing her lips to mine, so soft, so sweet, then pressing harder. I lean into the kiss, drawing strength from it. It's over too soon, like a lot of things.

Hannah gives me a mysterious smile, then backs away, dark eyes gleaming.

I dig. It takes the better part of twenty minutes to excavate the prison. I could have done it faster, but I wanted to hold onto the moment. Right now, I'm the hero. Right now, Hannah needs me. But after... Who can say?

Finally, the wards are uncovered. They're similar in appearance to the ones we dealt with before, but far more complicated. I have no idea if I can break them. I look up, a hundred feet or more to the top of the hole I've dug. They're all looking down at me in anticipation.

"Got it!" I call up to them. "These wards are crazy."

"We're coming down," Hannah says. "Don't try to break them."

"What? Why not?"

"Just don't, all right?"

I shrug. Now who wants to draw things out? I guess I can't blame her. She wants to be right up close when Hades is released. I would too, if it were my dad. The thought calls up the image of Cronus, the dream-conversation we had...

'Once you see what Hades is really like,' my father had warned, 'once you see how badly you have been used by the Gods, then you will come to Cronus.'

He'd been trying to trick me, of course. Make me paranoid, like him. But as Hannah, Ares, and Cerberus come down the concave side toward the unearthed prison at the bottom, I begin to get a bad feeling. A shivery feeling like maybe Cronus knows something I don't...

The King of the Titans promised 'hard lessons,' and told me how hard they would be depended on me. Now there's nothing I can do but find out if my father was right.

# 35

---

## SOME THINGS CAN'T BE SACRIFICED

"WHY DIDN'T YOU WANT ME to break through?" I ask Hannah when she joins me at the bottom of the hole.

"Because brute force isn't always the answer. The prison could be trapped, or any number of things. Would you climb a mountain without studying it first? Knowing which is the best angle to ascend the peak?"

"Good point. OK, take a look." I step away from the center wards, the mystic symbols in the ceiling of the prison cell. I'd been standing close to them, but not quite on them, so Hannah was right. We shouldn't take any chances.

She squats down and studies the wards, brow furrowed in concentration. I can only imagine what she sees, because it's all witchy nonsense to me. Sprawling lines, some thick, some thin, some interlocking, some apart, and all in a language older than time. Some of the wards are engraved, some painted, while others appear to be burned or clawed into the stone. That's the other thing—the prison stone is different from the basalt that makes up the rest of the island. It's granite, thick and gray, like Cerberus' cell. It was obviously imported and buried here, covered over to make it blend in with the rest of the rock formations near the Cliffs of Pain.

"That's what I was afraid of," Hannah says as she finishes her inspection.

"So it is true," Ares says. "I had hoped you were mistaken, but nonetheless, I stand ready."

"What do you mean, you're ready? What are you two talking about?"

"The wards," Hannah explains.

"Yeah? What about them?"

"Cronus made them so they can only be broken in a specific way."

"Just tell me where to focus my energy. I'll get us through."

"No," Hannah says, "you won't."

"A sacrifice is required," Ares adds.

"Sacrifice? What kind of sacrifice? What the hell is going on? And how did you know and for how long?"

Hannah shrugs. "You know I talk to ghosts. Back on Earth, I'd summon them from Tartarus for help, for company, and to keep me informed of what was going on in Tartarus."

"Yeah, like Dr. Herophilos. I remember."

"Well, one of those ghosts worked in the quarry where the granite for the cells was being mined. It had to be mined in a certain way, an unusual way. So I had him look into it, and he told me Cronus used it in some special construction project years ago, at the end of the Gods War. Naturally, I was curious, and desperate for any leads into what he had done with my father. So I got the miner to give me the name of the project architect, and from him, I found out the granite was for cells—cells warded by Cronus himself."

"So you figured your father was in one of them."

She nods. "I didn't just suspect, Andrus. *I knew.* I got confirmation; the only thing I didn't know was who the other cells were for,"—she pats Cerberus on his nearest head—"or where the prisoners were being taken."

"OK, that makes sense. And the sacrifice?"

She looks from Ares to me, a look of sorrow on her face.

"You mean we have to sacrifice a God to break the ward?"

"Not just a God, Andrus. A mortal too."

"You mean Mark?"

She nods.

"Well, we're not going to do it! There's got be a way, some other way around this bullshit!"

"There isn't," Hannah says. "I did warn you not to bring him."

"Yeah, you did, but I thought you meant so he wouldn't get hurt, not so you wouldn't have to sacrifice him!"

Ares says, "It's not her. She can't be the one to do the sacrifice."

"What? So you mean you have to do it? Commit some kind of ritual suicide?"

The War God shakes his head. "It can't be me either."

I stare in shock at the two of them, shock and horror, as the truth dawns on me. "It's me," I say. "You want me to kill my best friend."

"It has to be a Titan who makes the sacrifice," Hannah says. "It has to be you, just like it has to be Mark, just like it has to be Ares."

"There are no other Gods left," Ares says. "No other mortals in Tartarus. And there's only one you. It has to be someone of Cronus' bloodline."

"I told you I needed you," Hannah says. "I just never said how much."

I back away from them, my "friends," the people I thought I knew. I back away from the quest, fate, destiny, and all the rest. "No! This can't be happening. I trusted you..." I trusted her with my heart, I trusted Ares with Mark's life!

Cronus was right.

*My father was right!*

Cerberus prowls forward, three heads nuzzling me, attempting to give comfort in his monstrous way. But the big dog is also whining, wanting me to free his master. I push the beast away, not hard, so he comes back and I push harder.

"Hannah! Will you please do something with your damn dog?"

The witch calls Cerberus to her side and he obeys reluctantly.

My thoughts race, my heart aches with hard lessons: *Anger. Betrayal. Confusion and despair.* But more than that, failure. Failure to protect Mark, the same way I failed to protect his sister, the same way

I failed my foster parents. And if I don't do this horrible thing—if I don't betray Mark—then my failure will apply to the whole human race.

"Andrus," Hannah begins, "I know this is hard, but—"

I cut her off with a snarl. "No, you don't know! You don't know shit! you don't know about me, or Mark, or mortals! You only know you, Hannah. You only know you want your father back. You don't care how it happens, you don't care who gets hurt."

"I care," she says, "but you're right. I care about my father more."

"You care about your father, sure, but about freeing him. What about me, Hannah? What about my father?"

"I don't understand—"

"Of course not, because you don't have to worry about becoming your father! *I do.* I have to worry about becoming just like Cronus, or worse! And I won't do it. I can't do it, even if it means quitting the quest. Some things can't be sacrificed."

Hannah and Ares take a step toward me, and I can't let them. Can't let them force me, or convince me, or get anywhere near me. I say the secret code Mark and I invented to free him from his possession: *"Aristea! Aristea! Aristea!"*

Both Olympians stop moving: Hannah in confusion, Ares in pain. The War God doubles over, clutching his sides as if to keep his divine essence locked inside.

"Cousin!" Hannah cries in alarm. "Cousin, what is it?"

"The vessel... fighting for control..."

Hannah whips her pale face toward me, anger flaring. "Andrus, what have you done?"

"A little magic of my own. An exorcism."

Ares stumbles to one knee, still bent over, still struggling to possess Mark.

"War has no friends," I tell him coldly, "only allies. Our alliance is over!"

Ares screams, head rising, neck muscles bulging, going taut. His red-gold energy pours from Mark's mouth. The emptied body collapses and looks dead.

# 36

---

## DEATH'S WAITING ROOM

I RUSH TO MARK'S SIDE. Hannah yells—curses at first, then what sounds like a spell. Cerberus growls. I don't pay attention to either of them. I only care about Mark, that he's alive and all right.

I shake him until his eyes open, then shake him again when he doesn't respond. Finally, he says, *"Ouch."* It's one word, but it's a start.

"Mark, buddy! You OK?"

He half-nods, half-groans. "What... what happened?"

I glare up at Hannah and Cerberus. "They wanted to sacrifice you! I used the code word to expel Ares."

Mark swallows, trying to form a response.

"Yeah, man!" I go on. "Can you believe it? And they wanted me to do it! They wanted me to kill you, buddy. I couldn't. I'm gonna get you back to Earth, to Lucy. We're getting out of this crazy Kingdom of the Dead!"

Hannah's muttering magic words, but whatever spell she's casting, it doesn't seem to be an attack. She's not even looking at me. Instead, she's looking up. That's when I see Ares isn't gone. His red-gold energy,—his divine essence—is swirling high above, not quite out of the hole. The witch is holding him here, preventing him from dissipating, disappearing off to wherever Gods go when they have nowhere else. It's not death, I guess, but some kind of Limbo.

*Death's waiting room.*

"Andrus!" Mark gasps.

"Yeah? What is it, man?"

"It's... OK."

"Of course it's OK! I told you, everything's going to be fine. We're going to get you well, and then we're going to march out of this place. We'll hitch a ride with Charon, or I don't know, we'll find some other way back if we have to."

"There is... no other... way."

"Of course there is! You just get some rest now. Everything will make sense soon."

"No," Mark says, his voice growing stronger. "I meant there is no other way. You have to do it, Andrus. You have to sacrifice me... me and Ares."

"No, I don't! You're delusional. You'll snap out of it. You'll snap out of it, all right, and some day, we'll both have a good laugh about this... The crazy time you asked me to kill you."

"Not kill," Mark stresses, *"sacrifice."*

"Call it whatever you want, I'm not doing it! Get that through your head. I'm not doing that to you. End of story."

"The story really will end if you don't," Mark says. His eyes flick to Hannah. "She can't hold Ares' energy long, and if she loses it, she'll never get it back. He'll be gone, and then Hades will never be free, and neither will you..."

"No." It's all I can think to say. I hold Mark tighter. "No! It's not gonna go down that way. I'm not a monster! I'm not evil, not Cronus... Don't you see? If I do this thing, I'll be just like *him*. It's only a matter of time. This is what he wants... He wants to twist me, tear me from my friends till I have nothing left but him."

"You won't," Mark says. "You won't be like him. Believe that!"

My vision blurs as I fight back tears. Maybe this is part of being the Bridge Between Worlds, crossing from the old me to the new.

"Let me do this," Mark whispers, "for Lucy, for you, for everyone!

Let me save the world my own way."

"No." I say it again, but I can feel the fight going out of me. I know he's right. As much as I don't want him to be, as much as I want this whole thing to go away, I have to face the terrible truth: I'm going to sacrifice my best friend and my teacher to bring Death into the world. To bring Death back, so Life has a chance to mean something again. "All right," I say. "All right, damn you! I'll do it, but this is your decision, not mine!"

Mark nods. "It is. It's good you asked. Good you tried to stop it, but now it's time. Hannah can't hold Ares much longer..." He turns his head toward her. "I'm ready," he says. "I want this."

*"Do it,"* I hiss at the witch. "Do it, damn you! Do it now!"

Hannah, sweat dripping, hair plastered from the strain of holding the War God, redirects the divine essence down.

"Goodbye," Mark says, "and thanks."

"For what?" I ask.

He grins. "Letting me die a hero."

Red-gold mist funnels into Mark's mouth. His eyes roll up in his head, his body convulses, and then Mark is submerged inside himself. Possessed. It is not Mark, but Ares who rises. Ares who says, "It seems our alliance is not broken after all."

I get to my feet, feeling like I'm in a dream. No, not a dream—a nightmare, but one that will be over soon. "How do you want me to do it?" I ask them. "Sword? Stone? What?"

"It should be your choice," Hannah says. "The only requirement is their blood and energy must be spilled over the central ward."

Ares hands me his golden sword, the twin to the blade I'm carrying. "Here, I won't need this where I'm going."

I take the blade, studying the exquisite, otherworldly workmanship, and wonder how many have died on its edge, the way I feel like I'm dying now.

"It's fitting I should die by my own weapon," Ares says. "He who lives by the sword, dies by the sword. There's poetry in that."

"You should have told me."

"In my own way, I did."

He's right, but I didn't listen then, and I don't want to listen now. I plunge the sword into Ares' chest. Wanting this to be over.

Mark's blood spills. Ares' energy spills. Over the ward. Into it. *Slick and shimmering.* The ward absorbs it all. The ward eats it up. It eats it up and chokes on it. Cracks appear. Fine lines at first, like wrinkles, then widening, spiderwebbing in all directions. There's a rumbling in my ears, a hole in my heart—a hole where agony lives, and can never die.

My father did this to me.

*My father did this for me.*

It's all so horrible... As awful as any of the myths and legends about the Gods and Titans I was taught in school. Only I'm living it. I'm living my own legend and someday, someone will teach a class about me, and what will they say? That Andrus Eaves was a hero? That he did what he had to, no matter the cost? Or that he was just like his father, selfish and cruel?

*Every man's hero is someone else's villain.*

Hannah and Cerberus scramble back from the chaos, but I just stand there. I made this happen, I should own it, and maybe, if I'm lucky, I'll die too. I've never lived in a world with Death before. Will it be any better than the world we have now, or just a different kind of pain?

I look up, perhaps for the last time, and see Hannah's raven circle, see the gemstone "stars" in the cavern ceiling like a million judging eyes. What I don't see is the prison under me explode. I don't see it, but I feel it. In a way, it's like those souls in the river... the souls submerging themselves for their sins. Only there is no flame here, only freezing dust, smoke, and shadow—the shadow of Hades, God of Death, King of Tartarus.

"Free!" the ancient God shouts in a voice like a tomb. "I am free! Let the people die, let the Titans tremble, for Hades shall have his revenge!"

It's true. Hades is free, and Death is free, but I am not. I'm a prisoner of all that I've done, and all that I'll do, from this moment to eternity.

# AFTERWORD

A LOT OF PEOPLE think sequels are easy, and maybe they are if the author decides to "phone it in," but that's not the way Dan and I work. We knew we had something special with *Titan*, so for the sequel, we wanted to make everything bigger, better, wilder. We had to deepen the characters. *We had to make them even more real.*

One of the things that made writing Book 2 so hard is that it takes place in a new location, Tartarus, so we had to world-build almost entirely from scratch! That meant research. A lot of research, into everything from locations to mythical creatures, even the type of rocks. Not to mention magic and the afterlife...

*Kingdom of the Dead* sends our series in a more traditional fantasy direction, but we want to assure you *The Gods War* is still an urban fantasy series. Book 3 will return our heroes to Earth and the New Greece Theocracy. There will be plenty of shocks and surprises along the way, since they're not out of Tartarus yet... What will Hades do? How will Cronus respond? You can be sure Andrus and Hannah will be caught in the middle as The Gods War rages on. Don't miss the next exciting book in the series!

— DANIEL MIGNAULT & JACKSON DEAN CHASE

# GLOSSARY

- **Anton:** A ruthless inquisitor who serves the New Greece Theocracy. He raped Mark's sister Lucy and tried to capture Andrus and Mark to feed to Cronus. Before he could succeed, Lucy stabbed him, allowing Andrus and Mark to escape. First seen in Book I.
- **Archieréas:** The high priest of Cronus who serves as administrator, pope, and president of the New Greece Theocracy. The current office holder is Enoch Vola. Pronounced Ar-CUH-ray-us. First seen in Book I.
- **Centaur:** Monsters that are half-horse, half-goat-man, with the horns of a ram. They serve as cavalry for the Titans. First seen in Book I.
- **Cerberus:** The former guardian of the gates of Tartarus, Hades' faithful three-headed monster dog. Pronounced Ser-BUR-us. First seen in Book II.
- **Charon:** Ferryman of the Dead, Deliver of Souls to Tartarus. He looks like a robed and bearded mummy, a skeleton wrapped tight in leathery skin. Charon speaks through telepathy. First seen in Book I.
- **Cronus:** King of the Titans, father of the Greek Gods. His

symbol is the Unblinking Eye. Pronounced CROH-nus.
First seen in Book I.

- **Cyclops:** A one-eyed giant used as heavy infantry by the Titans. Plural: Cyclopes. First seen in Book II.
- **Day Patrol:** Armed bands of human warriors that serve as police; they answer to the priesthood.
- **Democ:** A centaur and member of the Night Patrol. Brother to Nessus and Ruvo. First seen in Book I.
- **Gaia:** The Earth Mother. She created the Titans with her lover, Ouranos, the Sky Father. Pronounced GUY-yuh.
- **Gyges:** One of the Lesser Titans and one of three brothers, all giants with fifty heads and a hundred hands who guard the gates of Tartarus in Cerberus' absence. Pronounced GUY-ghez. First seen in Book II.
- **Gods War:** The final battle between the Greek Gods and Titans in which the Gods lost and were either killed or imprisoned in Tartarus.
- **Hades:** Greek God of Death and the Underworld, older brother of Zeus. His symbol is the bident (a two-pronged trident). His imprisonment at the end of the Gods War prevents mortals from dying, but not from aging or becoming diseased or injured (see zombie). Pronounced HAY-dees. First seen in Book II.
- **Harpy:** Monsters that are half-woman, half-bird, with the head and neck of a vulture. They serve as scouts and aerial shock troops for the Titans. First seen in Book I.
- **Herophilos:** A ghost and great doctor in ancient Greece responsible for many advances in medicine. However, this knowledge was gained by performing autopsies on live prisoners. First seen in Book I.
- **Losers:** A popular insult, and also the name of the lowest free caste in society. Most slaves live better.
- **Loserville:** Slang for the run-down, economically challenged area of East Othrys; its population are "Losers."

- **Lucy Fentile:** Mark's sister and Andrus' love interest. She stabbed Inquisitor Anton at the end of Book I to allow Mark and Andrus to escape the Inquisition. Anton clubbed her over the head with his mace and her current fate is unknown. First seen in Book I.
- **Nessus:** A cruel centaur and captain of the Night Patrol in Othrys. He holds a grudge against Andrus for trying to trick him and making him look bad to his superiors. His brothers are Democ and Ruvo. First seen in Book I.
- **New Greece Theocracy (NGT):** An oppressive regime built on what's left of America after the Gods War destroyed much of the rest of the world. The NGT runs along what was the west coast, from Washington state to California. The Titans used their magic to transform its climate to match that of the Mediterranean.
- **Night Patrol:** Armed bands of human-hating monsters that enforce the after dark curfew. Mostly made up of centaurs and harpies.
- **Othrys:** Capital city of the NGT; named after Mount Othrys in Greece, birthplace of the Titans and their former capital on Earth. Previously known as Los Angeles. Pronounced AWTH-rees.
- **Ouranos:** The Sky Father. Lover of Gaia, the Earth Mother. Devoured by their son, Cronus. Pronounced OR-raw-nos.
- **Pankration:** A form of mixed martial arts practiced by the warriors of the NGT. It combines boxing and wrestling, with lots of takedowns, chokes, and joint locks.
- **Rich-O:** Loser slang for the wealthy caste.
- **Ruvo:** A centaur and member of the Night Patrol. Brother to Nessus and Democ. First seen in Book I.
- **Tartarus:** The Kingdom of the Dead, once ruled by Hades, now by Cronus. Another dimension that connects to Earth through underground portals.
- **Zeus:** King of the Gods, ruler of Mount Olympus, brother

of Hades, and son of Cronus. His symbol is the lightning bolt. Pronounced ZUICE.

- **Zombie:** A person who should be dead but isn't, often with a traumatic brain injury. Zombies are doomed to wander in pain for eternity—or until Hades is freed from his prison. First seen in Book I.

---

## A SUPER-IMPORTANT MESSAGE FROM THE AUTHORS

Dɪᴅ ʏᴏᴜ ᴇɴᴊᴏʏ ᴛʜɪs ʙᴏᴏᴋ?

If you did, **please write a review** of *Kingdom of the Dead* to help other readers discover the magic of *The Gods War* series. Thank you!

— Dᴀɴɪᴇʟ & Jᴀᴄᴋsᴏɴ

---

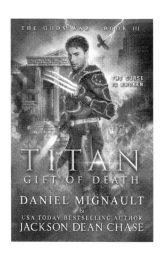

The adventure continues in
GIFT ᴏғ DEATH
Tʜᴇ Gᴏᴅs Wᴀʀ, Bᴏᴏᴋ III
— *available July 27, 2018 in eBook and paperback* —

# ABOUT DANIEL MIGNAULT

Daniel Mignault started in the entertainment industry from a young age as an actor and model surrounded by worlds of fantasy and imagination.

As Daniel grew older, he found his passion change from being in front of the camera to creating the stories and characters he once played. Now a full-fledged writer, Daniel is ready to bring his stories to life.

*Titan* is his debut novel.

## CHECK OUT DANIEL'S FILMS AND VIDEOS

Visit his IMDB page or YouTube channel.

*For more information:*
www.danielmig.com
www.imdb.com/name/nm3693355

amazon.com/author/danielmignault

facebook.com/danielmignaultauthor

twitter.com/DanielMignault

instagram.com/officialdanielmignault

## ABOUT JACKSON DEAN CHASE

JACKSON DEAN CHASE is a USA TODAY bestselling author and award-winning poet. His fiction has been praised as "irresistible" in *Buzzfeed* and "diligently crafted" in *The Huffington Post*. Jackson's books on writing fiction have helped thousands of authors.

FROM THE AUTHOR: "I've always loved science fiction, fantasy, and horror, but it wasn't until I combined them with pulp thrillers and *noir* that I found my voice as an author. I want to leave my readers breathless, want them to feel the same desperate longing, the same hope and fear my heroes experience as they struggle not just to survive, but to become something more." — JDC

*Get a free book at* www.JacksonDeanChase.com
jackson@jacksondeanchase.com

amazon.com/author/jacksondeanchase

bookbub.com/authors/jackson-dean-chase

facebook.com/jacksondeanchaseauthor

instagram.com/jacksondeanchase

twitter.com/Jackson_D_Chase

A JON WARLOCK SUPERNATURAL THRILLER

# WARLOCK RISING

USA TODAY BESTSELLING AUTHOR
## JACKSON DEAN CHASE

# WARLOCK RISING SNEAK PREVIEW
# CHAPTER 1

FULL NOVEL RELEASES SEPTEMBER 14, 2018

IT WAS ANOTHER BLACK FRIDAY in the Emerald City. November rain beat my spirit like a punch-drunk fighter from an angry sky. I sat in my office in the old Mireton Building overlooking Pioneer Square. It was a pile of bricks left over from a few centuries ago when the city was new. The rent was cheap, the downstairs windows barred. It was that kind of building in that kind of neighborhood. The Mireton was ugly, sure—there was no disputing that—but it had a certain character. Some might say charm. It also stood on a ley line, which is fancy wizard-talk for a naturally occurring magical power source. Basically, my office came with the magical equivalent of free wi-fi.

I'd been working out of the Mireton for five years. The past few hadn't all been rosy though. The city had redevelopment plans for the area, and they'd begun by tearing down first one eyesore, then another. The two most recent casualties were on either side of the Mireton: the condemned Rent Rite Apartments and Pacific Star department store. The Pacific Star had been boarded up for years, but the city'd had some trouble convincing the last of the Mireton residents to vacate. Some of them had nowhere else to go—nowhere affordable, at least—and traded sleeping in their rent-controlled apartments for bedding down in rent-free alleys. Loft apartments had gone up in their place, though the new buildings had been slow to fill thanks to the economic downturn.

I took a sip of morning coffee, winced, and sighed. No Starbucks for me, just a bitter bargain brand. Straight black. I rolled my battered chair over to the enormous bay window that was the central feature of my top floor office. The dirty glass hadn't been cleaned in years, and was one of those things I'd been hounding the landlady about. The window had my name emblazoned across it:

JON WARLOCK
PRIVATE EYE

Of course, the words appeared backwards to me. They were meant to be read from the street, five stories below. There was a design element under my job description: the Eye of Horus. It was an ancient Egyptian symbol that was supposed to provide protection as well as good health. Symbols on their own are just that, and more to make the user feel better than provide any real benefit. I'd added it to the glass as part in-joke and part clue I wasn't your normal P.I.

But it wasn't just to be clever. Inside the pupil, too small to be seen from the street (and barely noticeable even up close), I'd inscribed a protection ward written in my own blood. I hadn't had a chance to test it yet, and I hoped I never would, but investing in a good ward is like having a good insurance policy: Better safe than sorry.

I rubbed my dirty sleeve against the even dirtier window and peered out. Seattle was still Seattle—wet, cold, and lonely. Above me, the sky was nothing but rain. Below, the street nothing but bums. Pioneer Square was crawling with them: the mad, the homeless, the damned. I was one of them once, before I came into my power.

The knock at the door startled me. There was a hesitation in the first two raps, then the next two were more forceful. A bill collector wouldn't have been so nervous. That meant it was a client.

"Come in," I said, rolling myself back behind my desk. I was prepared for a client, but I wasn't prepared for what walked through my door. To call this redhead beautiful would be an understatement. Her hair was flame-red, framing a flawless face.

"Are you Jon Warlock?" she asked. "The wizard?"

I sat a little straighter in my chair and tried to keep my eyes on her face instead of where they wanted to go. "That's me. Please, have a seat." I motioned to the guest chair across the desk and opposite mine.

Whoever this redhead was, she was no slouch at making a good first impression. She smiled, revealing even white teeth, and shut the door behind her. Crossing to the chair only took seconds, but she knew how to make each one count. *Lithe. Cat-like.* She sat, crossing her legs and smoothing her skirt.

Her perfume crept up my nose and made me forget my usual witty banter. It was all I could do to ask, "Um, how can I help, Miss...?"

She gave another of those coy smiles of hers and I realized my jaw was hanging open. I snapped it shut with an audible click.

"My name's Whately," she said. "Constance Whately." She seemed to be waiting for me to recognize the name, but not only was my mind drawing a blank, it was drawing a lot of other things too, most of them not fit to mention. "Of the Bellevue Whatelys," she added.

"Ah," I said. I wasn't much for keeping up with the social register, but it seemed to me I'd heard the family name before. They'd made their money designing software, maybe some kind of app, like so many of the new rich. Bellevue was definitely ritzy. I'd only been there once, for a sci-fi convention, and that had been decades ago. The only thing I remembered (other than getting Leonard Nimoy's autograph), was how clean Bellevue was. For a city, it hardly looked lived in at all.

I leaned forward, steepling my fingers and putting on my most serious expression. "How can I be of service, Miss Whately?"

She shrugged. "You're the detective. You tell me."

"I'm also a wizard," I replied, "but I won't be needing my crystal ball to guess why you're here."

"No?"

"No, besides, if I did use it, I'd have to charge extra." That got a small smirk from her, so I continued. "Let's see... Judging by your age, your appearance, and the fact that you picked me of all people, I'd say you're in trouble or you know someone who is."

"That doesn't take a genius," Constance said. "Perhaps I made a mistake coming here."

I chuckled. "Yeah, I get that a lot, but I never advertised I was a genius. Just a wizard."

"Not the only one in the book," she argued.

"That's true," I admitted, "so either you want a single man outfit who knows how to keep quiet or the Bloodstone Agency turned you down. Which is it?"

Constance frowned and sat a little straighter in her chair. "I require discretion, Mr. Warlock."

"I see." I turned toward her. "Well, I'm nothing if not discreet. So is this a missing persons case?"

"How do you know it's not a cheating husband?"

"You do know what you look like, right?"

She smiled briefly at the compliment before her expression darkened. "Yes, it's a missing person. My sister, Veronica, hasn't come home in days. It's not like her. My father and I are worried."

"And does your father know you're here?"

"No. Father wouldn't... well, he wouldn't approve, that's all."

"Of hiring a wizard?"

Constance shook her head. "A detective. I don't think he'd even understand the wizard part."

"Not many do. Have you reported your sister's absence to the police?"

"Not yet. Father and I are hoping to avoid any unwanted publicity."

"Of course. I'm assuming Veronica is an adult?"

She nodded. "My sister turned eighteen last week."

I guessed Constance's age to be in her mid-twenties, but she might have been thirty. It was hard to tell. Beauty like hers had a timeless quality. I cleared my throat politely and asked a harder question. "Do you think Veronica ran away from home or do you think she was abducted?"

Her eyes flickered before answering. "Does it have to be one? Can't it be both?"

I furrowed my brow. "You'd better explain that."

"Well," she hesitated, then continued, "She left the house on her own initiative, but I don't think she's being allowed to return. The people she's with—they're a cult."

Now things were beginning to make sense. There were plenty of cults in Washington state, some harmless, some not. Most were an offshoot of Christianity, some were Wiccan, and others worshipped darker things. The problem with any cult, of course, was their tendency not to want to let go of their members. Especially pretty girls. Or wealthy ones.

"A cult?" I asked. "What kind of cult?"

Constance shuddered, which like anything she did with her body, was a joy to watch. "They call themselves the Sisters of the Way. They're witches. They claim to be good—'white light' and all that— but it's just an act. I think they're after my sister's money. When she turned eighteen, she inherited a large sum."

"How large?"

"Large enough. Half a million."

I whistled and leaned back in my chair. I hadn't heard of the Sisters, but there were too many cults to keep track of and new ones sprang up every day. "What makes you think they're not sincere?" I asked.

"Veronica is young and impressionable, and not altogether right. In the head, I mean. She got into witchcraft about a year ago. Everything seemed fine at first, although she was acting a bit more eccentric than usual." Constance noticed the look I gave her and shrugged. "No offense."

"None taken. Magic attracts the eccentric and tends to magnify that quality in its practitioners. That doesn't mean we're not right in the head..."—and here I paused for dramatic effect—"just that we're attuned to a different wavelength. You can't open yourself to the mysteries of the universe without being changed. Some of us more dramatically than others."

"I wouldn't know about that," Constance said, "but I do know that my sister won't listen to anyone who isn't into the occult. That's the other reason I want to hire you; you speak the same language when it comes to all this funny business."

I forced a smile. The uninitiated often disparage the magically inclined, so I tried not to be offended. I tried hard because this was the second crack she'd made against my profession. Beauty can make a man overlook a lot of flaws the first time, but repeat offenses will eventually break any woman's spell. As far as Constance was concerned, I resolved to only give her three or four more chances before deciding I disliked her.

"So you want me to investigate this cult and find out what their intentions are toward your sister?"

"I don't care about the cult. I want you to bring Veronica home."

"That could be difficult. Your sister's an adult; she doesn't have to go anywhere she doesn't want to."

"Persuade her then. Make her see it's in her best interest."

"And if I can't? If she refuses to come with me?"

Constance shrugged. "Can't you force her?"

"I'm a detective, not a kidnapper." I could tell my answer wasn't to her liking, so I added, "What I can do is try to convince Veronica returning home would be in her best interest. To do that, I'll need to dig up some background on the cult. What do you know about them?"

Constance reached into her designer handbag and handed me a glossy brochure for the Sisters of the Way. I skimmed it, surprised by the professionalism of their marketing pitch, but what really stuck out was their talk about exorcism. Apparently, they promised protection from demonic forces and evil spirits. That wasn't the only thing they promised, but it was the one part of the sales pitch that someone —I assumed Veronica—had circled in red ink. I scratched my chin with my free hand, looked at Constance, then back at the brochure.

The Sisters of the Way had a West Seattle address on Alki Point. OK, that meant a trip across the bridge, maybe twenty minutes assuming I could avoid rush hour and holiday traffic.

I held up the brochure. "Mind if I keep this?"

Constance nodded.

"I'm assuming you found this in Veronica's room? That she's the one that circled the stuff about exorcism?"

"Yes." A pained look came over my new client's face. "She's delusional, Mr. Warlock."

"Call me Jon."

"Fine. Here's the thing, Jon..."

I arched an eyebrow and waited.

"My sister got drunk one night last week and told me she got in over her head with all her conjuring or whatever. She talked about demons stalking her; she thinks she's possessed."

"Is she?" It was a fair question, but I didn't expect a fair answer, just the usual close-minded talk of schizophrenia or bipolar. Not that those things weren't real and far more common, but what most "normal" people failed to realize was that possession was real too. A person possessed by a ghost or demon could easily mimic the symptoms of mental illness.

"Of course not!" Constance snapped. "She's just confused, that's all. If my sister won't agree to come home, convince her to check herself into a hospital. A good one that knows how to evaluate people in her condition."

I was taken aback by the suggestion. "You mean a mental hospital?"

Constance sniffed at the word disdainfully. "I mean a facility where she can get help from *real* professionals, not from these... these charlatans! They're preying on her fear. You have to help her."

"I can try."

"You mean you'll take the case? Oh, thank you!" The redhead's whole face lit up. "You don't know what this means."

"Yes, I do. It means a thousand a day plus expenses."

# WARLOCK RISING SNEAK PREVIEW
## CHAPTER 2
FULL NOVEL RELEASES SEPTEMBER 14, 2018

PART OF ME WAS GLAD when Constance was gone. I'm an introvert and enjoy my privacy. Dealing with anyone in the real world drains me, but dealing with a woman—especially one that looked like Constance—took even more out of me. It's a complicated dance talking to clients, feeling them out, then negotiating my fee. She hadn't even blinked when I'd told her. She'd just reached in her handbag and handed it over, her fingers close to touching mine, then drawing away at the last second.

The bargain was made.

I picked up the money, fanned it, counted it again just for fun, then stuck it in my wallet. A thousand bucks! And that was just to start. I didn't much care for material wealth, though I appreciated the things money could buy—or buy off. Mostly, what I appreciated it for was what it represented: *freedom*. The freedom to be left alone. To not have to slave at some mindless nine-to-five that would kill my soul faster than any demon.

Freedom is important to wizards. Freedom from the reality the material world imposes on us, from bills and other nonsense.

I paused to lock up, then cast the minor protection ward I always used over the door. It was a few muttered words and mystic gestures that created an antipathy effect should anyone try to break in. Basically, it made them feel uneasy, like they were being watched, and included the telepathic suggestion, "This is a bad idea; there's nothing here." The ward stayed in effect until I returned or someone broke it, whichever came first. This had the added bonus of telling me if anyone had broken in, as I'd immediately know if it was still in place or not as soon as I touched the door.

There were bigger, badder wards I could have used, like the one I'd placed on the window behind my desk, but those required a lot more magic and a lot more time. Since I wasn't expecting an attack, I didn't see the point.

I took the birdcage elevator down. It was one of those turn-of-the-century contraptions that gave the Mireton Building its charm. The birdcage was only slightly faster than taking the stairs, but a lot less work.

During the descent, I checked to make sure I had everything I needed: the photograph of Veronica Whately that Constance had given me after agreeing to my fee, the witch cult brochure that had their address printed on it, my smart phone, keys, and wallet, right down to the half-eaten roll of breath mints. I popped one and closed my eyes, savoring the wintry taste and listening to the elevator's gears. I like white noise. There's something comforting about the hum and whir of machines. They do what they're supposed to. There's security in that.

I got off on the second floor and walked to the landlady's office. The building was owned by Agnes Mireton, an eighty-seven year old busybody. She had a shrewish disposition somewhere between salty and venomous, depending on how late I was with the rent. Right now, I was almost a month past due, so I expected her to be positively serpentine.

Maybe it seems ridiculous for a wizard to be afraid of an old woman, but I'm nervous around anyone who has power over me. Agnes Mireton had the power not just to verbally abuse me, but to evict me—something she'd threatened to do many times. What saved me was she'd have a difficult time replacing me. Half the building was vacant and not likely to fill up soon, if ever. Like I said, Pioneer Square isn't the best neighborhood.

I steeled myself, then knocked on the landlady's door.

Agnes answered on the third knock, the angry yips of her twin poodles, Fred and Ginger, annoyingly loud in the background. The landlady's long white hair was stretched back in a bun so tight it seemed to pull some of the wrinkles out of her face. "Well!" she snorted. "It's about time. You got my money, Mr. Wizard?"

I ignored her usual dig at both my name and profession. Instead, I opened my wallet and handed her nine of the ten bills my new client had paid me. "Sorry, Agnes. I've only got nine. I can have the rest in a few days."

Almost like she had a magic of her own, the landlady's beady eyes stared straight past my hand to the remaining hundred dollar bill poking out of my wallet. "Seems to me you got ten. You wouldn't be holdin' out on me, would you?"

"A sweet old lady like you?" I smirked. "Not a chance! It's just that I need this money to cover expenses."

"A thousand's half of your rent," Agnes retorted. "That extra hundred could pay your expenses, or it could buy you something even more precious."

"What's that?" I asked.

"My goodwill." Before I could blink, the old woman snatched the bill from my wallet.

"Hey!"

She stuffed my thousand dollars down the front of her blouse. "Hay is for horses! I got expenses too. This building don't run itself."

"It doesn't run at all," I said, but Agnes had already shut the door. The poodles kept yipping.

The problem wasn't just that building was old, but the very ley line that drew me to it had a tendency to draw other things. Things with less manners and personality than myself came to feed on the energy radiating from the basement. Basically, the building was a magnet for the supernatural. While the Mireton's low prices attracted people, they were just as quickly repelled by all the paranormal activity going on.

It even got to me from time to time. For example, shortly after I moved in, I'd walked into my office one night to find the ghost of a morbidly obese accountant sitting behind my desk banging away on an antique adding machine. It turned out the ghost was a previous tenant who'd died of a heart attack during tax season. His "unfinished business" was completing all the returns he'd left unfinished. Apparently, he just couldn't let his clients down, even in death.

I'd tried to ignore him at first, but the problem wasn't just that the ghost was sitting at my desk, but that he wouldn't shut up. He kept mumbling numbers and tax codes and banging away on his adding machine. Then he'd mop his forehead, clutch his chest and make gurgling noises. You wouldn't believe how long it took that guy to "die" each night.

I was finally able to get him to go into the light by convincing him it was an ambulance coming to take him to the hospital. The dead are stubborn, and nothing if not single-minded. You know when he bought that story? After he'd completed the last tax return and I promised to make sure his clients got them. Naturally, the returns were as ghostly as he was. They disappeared along with him when he went into the light.

There'd been a few other incidents just as annoying but far less amusing. The worst one was when a few demons tried to use the ley line to slip from their dimension into ours, and demons being demons, they hadn't been satisfied just escaping themselves. No, they'd tried to widen the portal and bring along a few thousand of their friends! I'd put a stop to that. Ghosts may not make the best tenants, but demons are even worse.

I wondered if Veronica really was possessed, and if she was, was it a by a ghost or a demon? Of course, there were other, even worse things it could be. Nameless alien horrors from beyond the stars, for one. The kind of things that could strip your sanity bare and leave you a helpless, gibbering wreck.

"Got change?" a voice asked. It belonged to a grubby man with greasy hair. Not even the rain could wash him clean.

"Got change?" the homeless man repeated. His voice was a broken record, his brain caught in a loop as fierce as any ghost's.

I handed him a quarter. "Sorry. The landlady already beat you to my bankroll."

"Landlady," the man echoed, as if I had it so lucky. This guy wouldn't last five minutes with Agnes. I left the man standing there to harass the next person to come along. Two blocks later, I was at my parking garage.

A plump seagull was strutting around my car picking at crumbs. I kicked it away. It squawked angrily, then flapped off. Those damn birds were a constant menace. If the rain didn't get you, the seagulls would. Their crusty white droppings were everywhere. Except on my car, and only because I'd cast an anti-bird shit spell on it.

I took a moment to appreciate my 1978 Pontiac Firebird Esprit with its copper mist paint job. It was my pride and joy, exactly like the car James Garner drove in *The Rockford Files*. I was always a shy, lonely kid growing up. Other kids came and went, but TV characters were my only real friends. The only ones I could understand; the only ones who never let me down. James Garner's wisecracking, hard luck character, Jim Rockford, was one of my favorites. In fact, Rockford was my inspiration to become a private eye. I knew detective work wouldn't be a glamorous life, but it would be an interesting one that would give me a chance to help people while putting my powers to the test.

I hadn't always lone-wolfed it. I'd tried working for the Bloodstone Agency my first years, apprenticing under old Rudolph Bloodstone, the head of the company, but his managerial style turned out to be more like Saruman than Gandalf, so I quit. That hadn't gone over too well, and I'd had a few run-ins with Bloodstone operatives over the years. There'd been a few nasty clashes, but we'd eventually settled into an uneasy truce. Which was pretty rare for a wizard war.

I climbed behind the wheel of the car and turned the key. The engine purred. It was time to pay the Sisters a visit.

# WARLOCK RISING SNEAK PREVIEW
## CHAPTER 3

FULL NOVEL RELEASES SEPTEMBER 14, 2018

THE SISTERS OF THE WAY were located in a modest, dark brown bungalow along the West Seattle waterfront. It was a nondescript location screened off from its neighbors by a high hedge and metal fence. Several well-placed trees further obscured the location from the street. Since it's generally bad form for a private detective to park directly across from a surveillance target, I had no way of seeing into the compound. Instead, I was parked a few doors down.

Waiting.

A lot of people think being a private eye is all fast-talk and throwing punches. They get that from movies and TV. The truth is most of the time, you're doing surveillance. Ask any cop; he'll tell you stakeouts suck. They're boring. You're sitting in your car eating bad food and peeing in bottles, hoping for something to happen. I'd been parked outside the Sisters' compound long enough to have done both.

I googled the Sisters on my phone. There was only one result. It led to their official website, but the site was bare bones, a simple landing page to "Sign up for membership information and important spiritual news." There were no pictures of the cult members or their leader, and no more information than was in their brochure.

I turned my attention back to the bungalow. From what I'd seen in my initial drive-by, the house was typical for the neighborhood. It was all one floor except for a small attic built into the sloping roof. The pillared veranda had a porch swing and barbecue. It even had Christmas lights. Like many homes in West Seattle, there was no driveway, so I had no way of knowing whether any of the cars parked along the street belonged to the witches or not. I made note of a black sedan and gray panel van as the likeliest cult vehicles. Constance had mentioned her sister drove a red Mini Cooper and had given me the license plate. Unfortunately, Veronica's car was nowhere in sight.

The other thing missing from the house was signage announcing the cult's name. The whole set-up was so damned normal it set off alarm bells in my head. Seriously, any witch trying this hard to be this normal had to be all kinds of messed up. I should know—I'd tried to be "normal" for years.

When you're as eccentric as me, pretending to be normal is like committing the slowest suicide ever. So if the Sisters really were witches and not the charlatans Constance claimed, they had to be *really* committed to put on this kind of act. Most cults wouldn't bother trying to blend in. They'd set up shop in some out of the way location that offered greater control over their members. Someplace that gave them room to grow. This bungalow did none of that. That told me either there weren't many members or else the cult kept its headquarters hidden elsewhere. Probably in some creepy forest where they could light bonfires and dance naked under the moon.

That made me think of Constance for some reason, and in a most impure way. That red hair, those green eyes, and all the rest. Without clothes. Without guilt.

Seagulls flapped and shrieked overhead, pulling me out of my fantasy. It was getting dark. I yawned, stretched, and decided to try a little magical snooping. I could have done it sooner, but it's slow and uses up a fair amount of energy—energy I might need later. That's why I preferred to do things the old fashioned way. The Rockford way. Only my butt was numb and I had nothing to show for it.

So I leaned back and closed my eyes. Concentrating. I slowed my breathing, getting into that quiet, meditative state that took me down, deep inside myself. The sound of the ocean grew dim, becoming part of me, the waves my heartbeat, the wind my breath. When I was well and deeply under, I gathered my energy and rose up, out of my body. I had to roll my astral form from side to side to wriggle out. Then I was sitting on top of my physical body.

Superimposed.

Invisible.

A living ghost.

I got up, my astral "head" poking through the Firebird's roof. There was no need to open the door; I simply walked through the car into the street. From my spine trailed my ghostly "silver cord," a kind of psychic extension used to reel myself back into my body to make sure my spirit couldn't get lost. It had an almost infinite length, expanding as needed, and no matter how far I traveled from my body, it never dragged on the ground. It just floated in mid-air.

The silver cord was extraordinarily strong as far as astral constructs went, but it wasn't unbreakable. Getting your cord cut was one of the risks of astral projection. A cut cord made it difficult to get back into your body. Fortunately, that kind of damage was rare on Earth. It was more of a concern the further you traveled into other dimensions, other realities. There were things out there that couldn't wait to chew through your lifeline, and others that fed on it.

A tricked-out monster truck passed through me as I stood in the street. Electric banjos filled the air. I felt a slight shiver from the contact and I imagine the driver felt the same, though he'd just crank up the heat and forget about it. If he'd been sensitive to the supernatural, he would have seen or at least sensed my "ghost" and swerved to avoid me. But the truth is, most people who drive monster trucks don't have much in the way of sensitivity—psychic or otherwise. That's because the more firmly rooted you are in the physical world, the less insight you have into the supernatural. It's like trying to be good at sports *and* philosophy. I'm not saying it can't happen, but it's rare.

I drifted across the street toward the bungalow. My senses were on high alert, probing for defenses or signs of counter-surveillance. I knew my chances of being spotted were slim if I kept my distance and didn't try to enter the house. About the only way one of them could see me was to be astral at the same time as me, which would be incredibly bad luck. I couldn't rule out the possibility, so I broadened my search to probe above the house and below the street. An astral sentry could be lurking anywhere. Fortunately, I sensed no one.

What I did notice was the plumbing under the house. One of the first things you learn as a wizard is that non-living spirits can't cross running water. The reason living spirits can is our physical bodies, which we're still connected to, contain water. There are other reasons you'll hear, such as water representing life and purity, but I'll spare you the metaphysics. All that matters is running water serves two essential purposes: keeping non-living spirits out, or keeping them in. That's how houses stay haunted. It's not because ghosts don't want to leave, it's because they can't figure out how. Now demons, on the other hand, they get it. That's why they eventually figure a way out of any location they're summoned to. They can follow you around like that for years. You move and they stop bothering you for a few hours, a few days, maybe even a few weeks. But sooner or later, they break out and find you again.

Most houses have a network of pipes under them that confuse the hell out of non-living spirits, but that's not what they're built for. This bungalow's pipes, on the other hand, had been carefully planned and arranged with spirits in mind. It was a perfect, unbroken defense of running water, like a psychic moat. I was impressed and wished whoever built the Mireton had thought of that.

So, what did this revelation mean? It meant that the people that designed the house knew what they were doing. It meant they were smart, which almost certainly implied they held a degree of magical power. They also valued their privacy; the running water acted as a 24/7 barrier against uninvited incorporeal guests. But not against me.

A related question—but one I had no answer for—was who built the house, how long ago, and was that person the current owner? That was a job for my physical self at the Hall of Records. Maybe I could even acquire a blueprint. I considered the idea briefly. That's what Rockford would have done, although he almost certainly would have tried bluffing his way into the cult with a fake business card first.

Being a wizard, and not much of a people person, I decided to forge ahead with my current plan. Times like this made me wonder if I was a detective playing at being a wizard or a wizard playing at being a detective. Maybe I was a little of both.

There was one more thing I noticed: the metal fence was made out of iron. Iron—poetically referred to as "cold iron"—was a well-known disruptor to non-living spirits. Again, it was something to do with iron representing blood of the Earth. Cemeteries were surrounded by iron fences to keep ghosts in and demons out. So the cult had a double barrier; one water, one iron. If the water ever got shut off, the fence would serve as a back-up.

Whistling the theme song to *The Rockford Files*, I stepped through the metal gate onto the driveway. I'd made it about halfway down when the song died on my lips. It turned out the cult hadn't limited itself to warding the property against the non-living, but against wizards too. I was staring down at a spirit trap that had been intricately disguised inside an ornamental design in the driveway. Just like the protection ward I'd placed inside the Eye of Horus on my office window. But unlike mine, which was created to keep things out, the cult had built theirs to keep things in.

I was doing my best "mime in a box impression" when the front door opened and the witch came out.

She cocked her head, gave me a grim smile, and said, "Hello, Mr. Warlock. We've been waiting for you."

I HADN'T BEEN EXPECTING the personal greeting anymore than I'd been expecting the trap. I wasn't just feeling stupid, I was feeling scared, but I knew better than to show it. Never reveal your weakness to predators. Never admit defeat. And when your back is really up against the wall, use compromise, flattery, and humor to talk your way out. It humanizes you.

"Neat trick," I admitted, forcing what I hoped was a good-natured smile at the witch. "No, I'm serious! I've seen a lot of traps, and you did a good job hiding yours. You added a cloaking spell, right? Otherwise, there's no way I would have blundered into it."

The witch didn't reply, just watched me. She was middle-aged with an angular, long-nosed face. She wore a simple black dress belted at the waist with a large gold buckle. Her hair was long brown, streaked with gray. She looked like the wicked witch from *The Wizard of Oz* morphed with a Thanksgiving Puritan. I estimated she had about as much sense of humor.

I cleared my throat. "Say, I know this looks bad—me doing a little astral trespassing—but we could both avoid a lot of trouble if you'd answer a few questions for me."

"Before or after I kill you?" the witch asked.

I gulped and tried not to squirm. "Oh, um, before would be fine. I'd hate to have to haunt you looking for answers. What say we call it a professional courtesy? You know, one practitioner to another?"

"No." She raised her hands to start weaving a death spell.

"Hey!" I tried again. "There's no need for violence. I didn't come here to hurt anybody, and I'm not interested in whatever your cult is doing."

The witch paused in her casting, but her thin face grew angry. "Cult? Cult!" she spat. "We're a coven. We *help* people!"

"Did I say cult? Sorry about that! It's, uh, an easy mistake to make. I mean, they both start with the same letter. Anybody could get them mixed up, especially under pressure."

Her body tensed. "Goodbye, Mr. Warlock." She wiggled her long, witchy fingers at me.

I wished my name was Dorothy and I had a house I could drop on her. As it was, I didn't have any way to stop the witch doing whatever she was about to do. The trap prevented me from casting any kind of attack or defense.

The front door opened and I saw two more witches appear with Veronica Whately between them. They hustled her past us toward the street while the first witch—the one I assumed was the leader—continued her spell.

"Veronica!" I yelled.

The girl turned in my direction, but there was no way to tell if she'd seen me since I was invisible.

The death spell materialized as crackling black energy. I saw it snake toward me, reaching for my silver cord with hungry, knife-like precision. With no way to dodge or dispel it, I only had one option: wake up.

It takes an expert a solid five, maybe ten minutes to become astral, and ideally, it takes just as long to return to your body. To settle in. I didn't have minutes. I had seconds, and that was only if I was lucky. Rushing anything is never optimal, and never more so when that thing happens to be magic or psychic in nature. But I tried it anyway, knowing it would hurt.

I braced myself, but even that didn't prepare me for the white-hot agony of the experience. Stars danced behind my eyes, whole constellations lighting up and dying, then blazing again. My entire body jerked and spasmed, heart pumping, brain seizing. I was in two places at once and then I was back inside myself.

Stunned.

Helpless.

But alive.

Through the haze, I saw the three witches and Veronica pile into a black sedan and screech away. The world spun. I tried to move my fingers, to reach for the keys and give chase, but my hand swam in and out of focus. I felt sick. I barely had time to yank open the door before I blew chunks. The wet pavement received my offering, then me as I slumped out of the car into blackness...

———

*Want to find out what happens next?*

Read the full novel of
WARLOCK RISING
by
JACKSON DEAN CHASE

*— Available September 14, 2018 in eBook and Paperback —*

SACRIFICE TO
SURVIVE

DRONE

BEYOND THE DOME BOOK 1

JACKSON DEAN CHASE

USA TODAY BESTSELLING AUTHOR

# MORE GREAT BOOKS TO ENJOY

## THE BEST URBAN FANTASY AND SCIENCE FICTION

EXCITING NEW NOVELS BY USA TODAY BESTSELLING AUTHOR

JACKSON DEAN CHASE

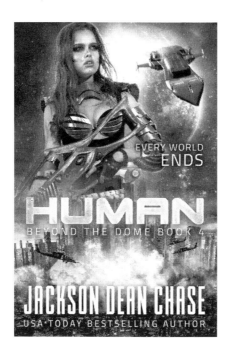

## BEYOND THE DOME

*Science Fiction Series*

- Book 1: *Drone* (releases August 3, 2018)
- Book 2: *Warrior* (releases August 10, 2018)
- Book 3: *Elite* (releases August 17, 2018)
- Book 4: *Human* (releases August 24, 2018)

## JON WARLOCK, WIZARD DETECTIVE

*Urban Fantasy Series*

- Book 1: *Warlock Rising* (releases Sept. 14, 2018)
- Book 2: *Warlock Revenge* (releases Sept. 21, 2018)
- Book 3: *Warlock Reborn* (releases Sept. 28, 2018)

---

## NEW NOVELS BY

## DANIEL MIGNAULT &

## JACKSON DEAN CHASE

## THE GODS WAR

*Urban Fantasy Series*

- Book 1: *Titan* (releases July 13, 2018)
- Book 2: *Kingdom of the Dead* (releases July 20, 2108)
- Book 3: *Gift of Death* (releases July 27, 2018)

---

Want to read exciting previews of these series and more?

*Get a free book at*

www.JacksonDeanChase.com

# SPECIAL FREE BOOK OFFER

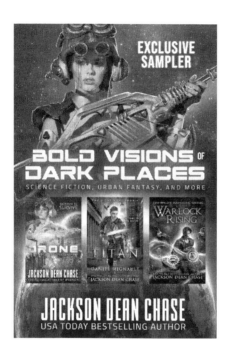

Printed in Great Britain
by Amazon